THE GEORGIAN BEEKEEPER

THE GEORGIAN BEEKEEPER

THE RYAN MADIGAN SERIES

Robert O. Morris

LEGACY PUBLISHERS

The Georgian Beekeeper

Book One of the

Ryan Madigan Series

Copyright © 2017 by Robert O. Morris.

Legacy Publishers
Virginia Beach, VA
www.legacypublishers.net
www.robertomorris.com

Library of Congress Control Number: 2016917480
ISBN 978-0-692-79713-6

Cover Image "Girl and Beehive" courtesy of www.lovethispic.com

First Edition 2016

Dedication:

This book is written in honor of the Nation of Georgia,
A beautiful country, blessed with magnificent people,
Including, for me, family members whom I deeply love,
And especially to the memory of one extraordinary woman,
Whose life is the inspiration behind this humble tribute.

CONTENTS

PROLOGUE   1

CHAPTER I   9

CHAPTER II   17

CHAPTER III   29

CHAPTER IV   41

CHAPTER V   51

CHAPTER VI   61

CHAPTER VII   73

CHAPTER VIII   85

CHAPTER IX   93

CHAPTER X   109

CHAPTER XI   121

EPILOGUE   131

AUTHOR'S NOTES   135

Disclaimer: The Georgian Beekeeper is a work of historical fiction. Whereas many of the events noted in this novella actually transpired, the author has taken a degree of creative liberty with history to adhere to the story line. Numerous characters introduced in this book did, or still do, actually exist. For those characters depicted in this novella who are still living, their names have been changed to protect their privacy.

Prologue:

She was "one of those rare people you only need to meet once to recognize that she is special," Madigan had written in his journal that day. The date of the journal entry was August 11th, 2006, and the location was the village of Choporti, Republic of Georgia, about 20 kilometers north of the ancient Georgian capital of Mtskheta.

Ryan Madigan was spending the day with his in-laws at a dacha owned by the brother of his father-in-law. Contrary to the heat and humidity of Tbilisi on a typical August day, the air was cool and fresh on this beautiful, clear day in the mountainous setting of Choporti.

On a business trip to Georgia, without his Georgian wife on this occasion, Madigan was picked up at his hotel in Tbilisi earlier that Saturday morning by his father-in-law. The 45-minute trip to the dacha was preceded by two stops, one to the vegetable market and the second to the lamb butchery to select food items for the day's "supra" (Georgian feast). Whereas the visit to the vegetable market was rather brief, the selection of the plump lamb to be butchered for the special event, under the expert, discriminating eye of Madigan's father-in-law, required some length of time.

Having finally arrived at the dacha, Madigan paid his respects to those family members he already knew and was introduced to those whom he was meeting for the very first time. This included his wife's paternal (and favorite) grandmother, Ksenia, about whom he had heard so much but never before had the opportunity to meet. Although she was just a few weeks short of her 83rd birthday, Madigan was immediately struck by the youthful radiance and intensity of her eyes, and the warmth of her welcoming smile.

Although Madigan had numerous questions that he had wanted to ask Ksenia, his inquiries had to wait until he had satisfactorily answered all of her many questions about her favorite granddaughter, and how she was faring in the United States. Since they had gotten married in the USA only 15 months prior, Madigan's wife had not yet been back to Georgia to visit her family since the wedding, so Ksenia wanted to hear about everything about her granddaughter and how she was doing.

The love and reverence that Ksenia felt for her granddaughter was clearly evident; she shed a few tears (perhaps due to happiness that her granddaughter was doing well, but more likely due to the fact that she missed her dearly) as Madigan filled her in on all the details. In addition to her inherent warmth, Madigan was equally impressed by the obvious intellect and wisdom that Ksenia exhibited during the lengthy conversation; despite the fact that she had lived in a rural village much of her life, Ksenia was clearly endowed with a unique gift of intuition and wisdom rarely bestowed on normal human beings.

This Saturday afternoon supra lasted, in good Georgian tradition, until well into the late evening hours; the "Tamada" (traditional Georgian toastmaster for the supra) on this occasion was the host, David, his father-in-law's brother. In keeping with timeworn Georgian tradition, David managed to raise more than 30 toasts in honor of nearly every possible recipient within the realm of Georgian human reality. This was all well and good, and certainly added to the festivity and gravitas of the event, but supra toasts tend to be both rather frequent and large in quantity, and therefore usually lead (particularly for non-Georgians) to some degree of inebriation. Nevertheless, a grand time was had by all, and Madigan departed the dacha that evening with a feeling of warmth and sincere gratitude that he had spent quality time with his wife's family, and especially that he had finally had the opportunity to meet grandmother Ksenia.

Returning to his hotel following the supra, Madigan reflected on his conversations with Ksenia; she had told him much about their family history, and about life during the challenging years of the 20th century, and Madigan felt privileged to hear her story. His wife had told him much about her grandmother, however Madigan had not previously understood how simply extraordinary Ksenia's life history had actually been.

* * * * *

Ryan O'Rourke Madigan liked to joke that he was born with three last names, which was factually pretty much the case; at least they were names of prominence within the Irish American community, which was indeed a source of pride for him.

Madigan was born on August 15th, 1971, in Chevy Chase, Maryland, a wealthy suburb of Washington, DC. He was the son of a 3rd generation US Military Academy graduate, Patrick Joseph Madigan, class of 1969, who broke the tradition of West Point graduates at the time by joining the US Army

Special Forces following graduation. Unfortunately, Captain Madigan was killed in action in 1973 "officially" noted in Southeast Asia, which Ryan later discovered was in Laos.

Ryan's mother, Mary Ellen O'Rourke, was a beautiful debutante from a well-to-do Chevy Chase family, who had made their name and fortune in the Washington real estate market. Mary Ellen had been raised in reasonable affluence, attended the prestigious Holton Arms School during her high school years, and later attended and graduated from Smith College in 1970. While at Smith, Mary Ellen attended a formal dance at the US Military Academy, where she first met a handsome young cadet, Patrick Madigan. It was love at first sight, and Mary Ellen and Patrick dated (at least as much as a USMA education allowed) throughout their college years. They were married in 1970, soon after her graduation from Smith, and Ryan was born one year later. After Captain Madigan's death in 1973, with Ryan being a mere 2 years old, Mary Ellen decided to enter her father's successful real estate company, and embarked upon a life as a single mother. Although she was a beautiful and well-to-do widow, and the recipient of a great deal of male attention and interest, Mary Ellen never remarried, and devoted herself entirely to her real estate business and to her only child, Ryan.

Ryan spent nearly his entire adolescent life living at home in Chevy Chase, both while at Georgetown Preparatory School and later following his enrollment at Georgetown University. Although Ryan had shown some interest in following in the family tradition to attend West Point, his mother, having lost her husband in action, was strongly against it. As a result, Ryan acquiesced to his mother's preferences and enrolled at Georgetown to pursue a degree in Foreign Service; this still answered Ryan's personal desire to serve his nation, albeit in a potentially less risky manner, which suited Mary Ellen just fine.

Growing up, Madigan was always one of the most popular boys in his school community. He was an extremely handsome young man, and one of the better athletes in his class, yet his genuine and engaging personality was the magnet that earned him a wide circle of friends. Although he was especially popular with the girls, Ryan concentrated his attention on his studies and sports; at Georgetown Prep, he was a star running back on the football team, and also excelled at track, specializing in the sprint events. Madigan grew up a devout Catholic, and even gave serious thought to becoming a priest one day, although this was not to be in his future path.

Due to his prowess in football, Ryan drew significant attention from a number of major college football programs, but his heart was set on attending Georgetown University; he liked their academic reputation, and, full truth be told, he wanted to stay close to home, and his mother. Ryan simply could not justify going to a college too far from home, since he understood how much his mother emotionally needed him to stay close. Ryan enrolled at Georgetown in 1989, where he excelled in his studies and played on the university football team; although Georgetown played at a Division III level in those days, it was a good football program, which he enjoyed, and it did not detract too much from his academic pursuits.

Madigan loved the Foreign Service program at Georgetown, highly regarded as one of the best in the nation. He had developed a strong interest in the history and realities of the Cold War, so his foreign language concentration within the Foreign Service program was Russian; Madigan had a natural affinity for foreign languages, at which he excelled. He had studied French at Georgetown Prep (a language in which his mother was fluent), and he also studied German as a second language at Georgetown. Ryan easily passed the challenging Foreign Service examination in his junior year at Georgetown, and he would have readily been accepted by the US Department of State to become a Foreign Service Officer; however, much to his mother's chagrin, he ultimately decided to follow his family legacy and joined the United States Army. Like his father before him, Ryan had his mind set on joining Army Special Forces, and to wear the "Green Beret."

Chapter I:

Ksenia Kolumbegovi was born on September 5th, 1923; she was the daughter and oldest child of Giorgi Kolumbegovi and Zina Museliani, and, from the moment of her birth, she was the apple of her parents' eye.

The marriage in 1921 between Giorgi and Zina had, in the tradition of the day, been an arranged union between two good Georgian families. Both the Kolumbegovi and Museliani families had a lengthy lineage in the history of Georgia and South Ossetia, and the two families wanted to continue the strong traditional blood lines. Like many arranged marriages, the bond between husband and wife was built more upon mutual respect and the pragmatic need between two human beings to combine forces in order to better survive during difficult times.

During the 19th century, Georgia had given its political allegiance to the Russian Empire, which brought with it numerous historical consequences: these included Russia's participation in World War I, both against the European Allied powers and the Ottoman Empire; Russia's demise in WWI which gave rise to the Russian Revolution; the abdication of the Tsar, and the establishment of the Union of Soviet Socialist Republics; and, following a brief period of Georgian Independence between 1918 and 1921, an invasion by the Red Army to bring Georgia into the fold as a member of the USSR. Such were the times when Giorgi and Zina joined their hands in marriage to face the challenges of the world together.

Giorgi had been born in 1896 in the village of Lopani, located near the Georgian border with South Ossetia. Like most Georgian boys living in a rural environment, Giorgi's life was dominated by school and the many requirements of life on the farm; because he was the oldest male son, he was given the primary responsibility for watching and herding the flock of sheep that belonged to the Kolumbegovi family. Once he reached the age of 17 in 1913, Giorgi spread his wings and moved to the capital city of Tbilisi in search of life in the big city and urban adventure.

Once in Tbilisi, Giorgi found a construction job working with the city administration. This employment was short-lived, however, since Russia entered World War I in 1914; he was soon drafted into the Tsarist Army, and assigned to the Russian Caucasus Army. Following a modicum of combat training and preparation, Giorgi was deployed with the Caucasus Army to face the jihadist hordes of the Ottoman Empire; by late December, 1914, Giorgi's unit had reached the Turkish city of Sarikamish, where they dug in and prepared for the eventual assault from the Ottoman forces.

The winter of 1914 was especially brutal, and sickness and frostbite was of constant concern to the Russian, and Turkish, forces. For weeks, the Turks had been attacking the dug-in Russian forces in the area around Sarikamish, located in the mountainous area of northeast Turkey, near the Georgian border. On the eve of the main assault on the city, the Russians were already quite weary, cold and undernourished from months of deprivation and the frequent skirmishes with the Ottoman forces.

The Russians, weakened though they were, were well-supported with artillery and machine gun units in their trench positions facing the Turkish forces. When the final assault began on the evening of December 29th, the Russians unleased a brutal and effective defense, and largely decimated the Turkish forces before they could reach the Russian positions. However, the small number of Turk soldiers who reached the trenches fought bravely and incurred significant losses upon the entrenched Russian forces in brutal hand-to-hand combat.

For his part, Giorgi fought bravely throughout the assault. He held his position, kept firing his rifle repeatedly and was personally responsible for several enemy casualties. One of the few Turkish soldiers to reach the edge of the Russian trench engaged Giorgi face-to-face; before he could end this courageous Turk's life with several blows to the head with the butt of his rifle, Giorgi parried a bayonet thrust which still managed to pierce his thigh. As a result, once the Turks had withdrawn and the battle had ceased, he was taken to the medical tent for treatment.

Giorgi's wound was sufficiently serious to require that he be sent for additional medical treatment and rehabilitation at the Caucasus Army regional headquarters in nearby Batumi. There Giorgi spent several months recuperating from his wound and the pneumonia that he had suffered due to the harsh conditions; afterwards, he was reassigned to the unit in Batumi responsible for the defense of the city. Although the Turks conducted several attacks on Batumi over the course of the next 2 years, Giorgi's combat role was sporadic and comparatively minimal, and he survived the duration of his Army experience without any further major trauma. However, by the time he was discharged in early 1917, his experiences in the war had made a major impact upon his political point of view. Upon his return to Lopani, where he returned to help his family in their farming operation, he joined the embryonic Worker's Revolution Party and helped to pave the way for the revolution to come.

It was during this period in Lopani, in 1920, that he met Zina and the plans for their marriage were arranged. Zina Museliani was the oldest of three children in her family; she was a very caring and giving child, and she was conscientious in helping to raise her two younger brothers, Vasili and Ivan. At the time she first met Giorgi, Zina had just turned 17; he was already 24. Zina was a pretty, yet quiet and introspective young lady; she had spent all of her life in the rural environs of Lopani, and she was attracted by the prospect of marriage to Giorgi, a strapping, more worldly, war hero. She envisioned a much more exciting existence with him, and she was intrigued by the active and important role that he was playing in Georgia's new revolutionary movement. Giorgi seemed exciting to her, and, although she did not really feel overcome with emotional love, she felt secure in his presence and optimistic for what the future might hold.

Giorgi and Zina were married in Lopani in 1921. By this time, although Georgia declared Independence from Russia in 1918, the country had eventually succumbed to pressures from Moscow and the Russian Revolution, and had officially become a member of the USSR. Ksenia was born in Lopani in September of 1923, and her sister, Lyuba, was born one year later. After Lyuba was born, Giorgi moved the family to Tbilisi where he began work with the railroad as a welder, a position that he held for the subsequent 32 years; he also continued his work in the Communist Party and he steadily rose in influence within the Party hierarchy.

Throughout his working years, Giorgi always remained loyal to the party, and faithful in his efforts to contribute to the common good for the people of Georgia and the USSR. Zina remained loyally by his side, spending all of her time supporting Giorgi and raising their two daughters, until her untimely death. Zina's younger brother, Ivan, with whom she had always been close, had been falsely accused of desertion from the Army; he was seized and sent to the Soviet gulag in 1937 and eventually disappeared amidst the horrific Stalin purges. Zina never recovered from the despair she felt from the loss of her beloved brother and the betrayal that she felt from the Soviet system; weakened by poor health and emotionally distraught, she passed away in 1939.

* * * * *

Ksenia's formative years corresponded with very challenging times in Georgia; the early years of the USSR witnessed economic and political challenges, even in the capital, Tbilisi, where conditions were far better than in the rural areas of the country. Although food was sparse and living conditions were generally austere, the Kolumbegovi family lived comparatively well due to Giorgi's job with the railroad and his influence within the Party, which often led to obtaining goods that were largely unavailable to others.

Despite the difficult times, Ksenia experienced a happy childhood, largely spending the months of the school year in Tbilisi, which offered a vast array of cultural and social experiences; during the summers, the family would return to Lopani to spend time with Giorgi's family in the cooler environs of the mountains. There Ksenia developed a deep love of nature, as well as for, what seemed to her, the glories of farming. She envisioned the Kolumbegovi farm as a miniature version of the Garden of Eden. In her mind, God had created this miraculous environment where beautiful flowers bloomed uncontrollably, creating their panorama of vibrant color. This was where fruits and vegetables grew effortlessly, to provide everything her family needed to live; and where her animal friends created a harmonic symphony of music that soothed her soul, and made her feel at peace with the world. Although she fully appreciated the necessity of the long days, hard work and synergistic family effort that was required to keep the farm working properly, for Ksenia this was nothing more than an endeavor of love that she grew to cherish.

From her earliest childhood days, Ksenia played an active role on the Kolumbegovi farm, helping with the livestock, tending the garden, gathering wild flowers, and learning to help in the kitchen; she also enjoyed the simple pleasures of gathering together with the family after a long day, during the quiet evening hours. It was really the best of all worlds, and she expanded her range of interests significantly. She developed an insatiable intellectual curiosity for learning how things grew, and how to take full advantage of all of God's gifts that one found within nature.

When her summer sojourn was over, the days having flown by in a haze of frenetic activity, Ksenia returned to Tbilisi for the school year, where she attacked her academic subjects with the equal zeal and determination as she approached chores on the farm. She found that she possessed a high interest and aptitude for mathematics and the natural sciences, which would certainly serve her well in her future pursuits. Socially, being a very pretty, energetic and gregarious young lady, Ksenia made friends easily, and she displayed an inherent tendency to evolve into a leadership role amongst her circle of friends. Although she was not the most beautiful girl in Tbilisi, nor the smartest student, Ksenia was the one child to whom everyone was drawn magnetically and simply wanted to be around.

The childhood and teenage years, spent between Tbilisi and the family farm in Lopani, were happy times for Ksenia, despite the general malaise that seemed to grip the country. Ksenia had been born soon after Georgia had been absorbed into the USSR, and had grown up during the difficult years of the 1920's and 1930's. This is the period when the Soviet Union struggled to introduce political and economic stability into an environment that had been turned upside down by world war, revolution, civil war, and the brutal dictatorship of Josef Stalin. Ksenia was a teenager during the years of Stalin's Great Purge, during which anyone perceived as being disloyal to Stalin or the Communist system was subject to imprisonment in the gulags or mysterious disappearance; it is estimated that more than one million Soviet citizens fell victim to Stalin's brutality during the mid-to-late 1930's, including Ksenia's uncle Ivan, her mother's brother. Uncle Ivan would not be the last family member to suffer such a fate.

Despite her mother's death the previous year, upon graduation from high school in Tbilisi in the summer of 1940, Ksenia decided to continue her studies and enrolled at the university to study accounting; this subject came quite easily to her, and she earned her certification within two years. In the meantime, just having endured the years of the Great Purge, the Soviet Union entered World War II in June of 1941; thankfully, following her certification in 1942, Ksenia had been assigned a teaching position in the rural village of Atotsi, near the border with South Ossetia. Since it was not far from Lopani, and Ksenia had travelled through the area on numerous occasions, she welcomed the opportunity to move back to the peace and quiet of the village, far from the drum-beating and political frenzy supporting the war effort.

Little did Ksenia know at the time, but Fate would soon intervene to make this move one of the most impactful in her short life.

Chapter II:

Mary Ellen Madigan had never truly felt disappointment in her son prior to this time. Ryan's revelation to her that he had decided to join the Army and to follow in his father's footsteps was devastating to her. Her feelings were not motivated by any negatives about her late husband, since Patrick Madigan was a larger-than-life, genuine hero in her eyes; it was only the memory of those darker-than-dark days when she first learned of Patrick's death in Southeast Asia that clouded her psyche. Since that time, she had devoted her entire adult existence to Ryan, and had sacrificed much for him; at first, it seemed like a slap in the face that Ryan was going against her wishes.

The mental transition for Mary Ellen did take some time, but, after numerous heartfelt, tearful discussions with Ryan, she came to understand his reasoning; after all, his primary motivation to join the Army Special Forces was in tribute to his father, who had been God-like in his eyes, just as he had also been in his mother's. In the final analysis, Mary Ellen came to the same conclusion that so many mothers have in the history of mankind; "my son needs to make his own decisions, and to find his own way, so may God's wisdom bestow him and His countenance shine down upon him."

It was during the early spring of his senior year at Georgetown when Ryan had finally reached the difficult decision that had tortured him for several years. He had come to the realization that his entire life's path and academic pursuits had been cleverly predetermined by his mother; this path would allow for a pursuit of national service, which, as she knew, was deeply embedded in Ryan's DNA, while still charting a compromise course that would still offer a modicum of personal safety. For the sake of his mother's peace of mind, Ryan had been willing to acquiesce to this long-planned career pursuit; but, in the final analysis, he needed to listen to his own heart and answer the same clarion call as the generations of Madigans who had preceded him.

So it was that, after having about two months for summer fun and frolic between graduation and his induction, Ryan officially entered the United States Army in early August, 1993. In his discussions with his Army recruiter, he was offered, and he chose, the path that would provide the opportunity to attend Officer Candidate School (OCS); based on his university degree and aptitude testing, this would allow him to earn his commission in the quickest possible time. First, however, there would be a 9-week Basic Combat Training course at Fort Benning, Georgia, which unfortunately commenced at the height of the summer heat and humidity. And, since the OCS class for which he was destined did not begin until late November, Ryan was offered the opportunity to attend the three-week-long Airborne School, also at Fort Benning, where he could earn his Jump Wings, a prerequisite to his desired Special Forces training.

Despite the debilitating heat of Ft. Benning during August and September, Basic Combat Training was a breeze for Ryan, as was the physically challenging Jump School. OCS offered a bit more of a challenge due to the very long hours of physical and mental harassment that the Officer Candidates faced every day for 12 long weeks; however, Ryan excelled in this environment as well and graduated among the top 5 Officer

Candidates in the class. Following OCS, per his "dream sheet" preference for assignments, Ryan was assigned to the JFK Special Warfare Center at Fort Bragg, North Carolina, where, for the next 14 months or so, he would endure the exhaustive Special Forces Qualifications Course training to become a "Green Beret" Officer.

Ryan completed the "Q Course" with honors and earned his Green Beret in May, 1995; by this time Madigan had been promoted to 1st Lieutenant and was ready for his first unit assignment. Since his primary foreign language skills, Russian, German and French, were best suited for the Special Forces Groups whose Area of Operations was Africa and Eastern Europe, including the Former Soviet Union, Ryan was assigned to the 10th Special Forces Group. This initial assignment with the 10th SFGA was at their home base at Fort Devens, Massachusetts, which was in the process of being relocated to Fort Carson, Colorado. As an enthusiastic, newly-arrived 1st Lieutenant, although happy to have achieved his goal of becoming a Special Forces Officer, Madigan was a bit disappointed to have been given an administrative position to assist with the relocation of 10th Group HQS. But, after all, everyone needs to pay their dues at some point; the "action" would certainly come soon enough.

Soon after the relocation of 10th Special Forces Group to Fort Carson was completed, Madigan got his first opportunity at an overseas deployment. In early December 1995, an advance element of the 10th Special Forces Group was deployed to Kiseljak, Bosnia-Herzegovina, in support of the first US combat forces to enter that country under NATO Operation Joint Endeavor. After several years of brutal civil war in

Bosnia-Herzegovina between the Bosnian Serbs, Croatians and the Bosnian Muslims, Operation Joint Endeavor was implemented as a peace enforcement mission, with the goal of separating the warring factions into their separate zones. Madigan had been assigned as Assistant S2 for intelligence and security with the Combined Joint Special Operations Task Force (CJSOTF) in support of several conventional multinational brigades.

In addition to his normal role as Assistant S2, due to his excellent Russian language capabilities, Madigan was also detailed as S2 Liaison Officer to the allied Russian Parachute Brigade; this entailed weekly briefings with that military unit, which he enjoyed, and, on the downside, the consumption of more vodka than he had ever previously imagined could be humanly possible. Otherwise, with the exception that a convoy in which Madigan was travelling came under sniper fire on one occasion, and another incident in which a nearby vehicle struck an IED, Madigan saw virtually no hostile activity during the year he was assigned to Operation Joint Endeavor. Nevertheless, Ryan's performance in Bosnia-Herzegovina was considered to have been highly effective and earned him respect from his superior officers. As a result, when the mission of the operation changed one year later, Madigan was reassigned to Special Operations Command Europe (SOCEUR) in San Vito, Italy, with the mission of training allied Special Operations Forces from the newly independent states previously under the dominance of the USSR.

With the onset of 1997, Madigan's life became a whirlwind of operational travel and military training activities in countries of strategic interest to the American government and NATO. Within a 2-year span, Madigan participated in Joint Combined Exchange Training (JCET) missions to the Czech Republic, Latvia and Macedonia, each lasting about one month in duration; JCETs offered the opportunity for operational units from each country to train together, and to benefit from the operational synergy each learned from the other. In addition to the JCETs, Madigan also had the opportunity to participate in SOCEUR Familiarization missions, each of 2-3 weeks in duration, to three other countries; these were Ukraine, Estonia and Georgia. The purpose of these trips was to assess the indigenous Special Forces units in terms of overall capability and future joint operations potential. As Fate would have it, the Georgia visit, a country that made quite a positive impression on Madigan, was to play a significant role in his life to come.

Madigan loved the continuous, sometimes frenetic activity involved with these missions, especially the planning, the execution and the after-action reports and analysis that each required. These post-Cold War years were important times, with the transition of many of the newly independent states from the Soviet to the NATO sphere of influence, and Madigan felt like he was playing an historically important role shaping the future of the free world. Like many who choose the challenging life of a Special Operator, Madigan was a romantic idealist who believed that he was on a sacred mission to help make the world a better place; moreover, he was having the time of his life, and he felt 100% fulfilled.

By late 1998, Madigan had earned a promotion to Captain, and he was assigned command of an Operational Detachment "A" (ODA), the standard operational unit of the Army Special Forces; it was composed of 12 men, 2 commissioned officers and 10 highly specialized non-commissioned officers. Soon thereafter, in early 1999, heavy fighting in the Balkans between ethnic Albanians and Serbians living in the province of Kosovo required another deployment of 10th Special Forces personnel into this war-torn region. Madigan commanded one of the ODAs that was deployed there, and it was here that he experienced his first combat. Due to Ryan's fluency in Russian, Madigan's team was attached to assist the Russian Brigade active in this area of operations; the ODA's primary role was for the collection of intelligence on the fighting between the Albanians and Serbs, and to support the Russian Brigade's operations. In the course of their time on the ground in Kosovo, Madigan's ODA was involved in several firefights, solely for self-defense, initiated by Serbian forces. Madigan's ODA also participated jointly with Russian units on weapons seizure raids, one which required calling in allied artillery support for the Russian operation. Historically, this was the first instance of US-Russian combat cooperation since World War II.

After 6 months of successful operations in Kosovo, Madigan's unit was recalled to their European base; having been overseas for the past 4 years, Madigan soon thereafter received orders to return to 10th Special Forces Group HQS at Fort Carson. Beforehand, Madigan took one month of leave stateside, in which he spent most of his time with his mother in Chevy Chase. Although he had corresponded with his mother almost on a daily basis while deployed in Europe, Mary Ellen had worried tremendously for her son's safety these past few years, and Madigan felt the need to spend some extended quality time with her.

While at home with his mother, Madigan celebrated his 28th

birthday; since graduating from Georgetown University 6 years previously, Ryan's life had been a whirlwind of activity and adventure. Despite her concern for her son's welfare, Mary Ellen was proud of her son's accomplishments and gratified that he seemed to love his work so much. Naturally, she was curious if Ryan would ever find a nice girl with whom to settle down and provide her with grandchildren, but, thus far, there were no serious candidates. As handsome and alluring as Ryan was to the world of females, he still had yet to meet anyone whom he considered marriage material; such a young lady would need to measure up well to his mother, a tough bill to fill, and such women were simply few and far between. Certainly, such an opportunity would come, but not just yet.

Upon arrival at Fort Carson, Madigan was given command of another ODA, and spent most of the next two years involved with training and "paying his political dues" as an officer assigned to stateside base duty. Whereas he had been energized and enthused by the challenges and occasional adrenalin rushes that life deployed overseas provided, garrison duty tended to test his patience and, on occasion, his self-worth; he simply did not feel like he was making a proper contribution to the nation while stateside, and he longed again for the action, or at least the constant potential for action, that he had experienced on his overseas deployments. Well, at the very least, Madigan would opine to himself, he was learning the fine art of being patient, a trait that his mother had (only somewhat successfully) endeavored to teach him; but, he would not need to exercise patience much longer.

* * * * *

Between 0630 and 0715 MDT, on the early morning of September 11th, 2001, Madigan and his team were in the midst of their daily 5-mile run; upon returning to their base station to shower and get ready for duty, they heard the shocking news that, while they were running, two airliners had flown into the World Trade Center. Along with everyone else in the civilized world, Madigan understood that life, as he previously knew it, would change from that moment forward; he also knew immediately that his lifelong desire to serve his nation had just manifested itself entirely, and he understood that the dice of his destiny had just been cast.

It was quickly determined that Osama bin Laden and his Al Qaeda terrorist network was behind the 9/11 attacks; Al Qaeda was being given safe haven in Afghanistan by the ruling Taliban. US Central Command was given the order from the White House to develop plans to eliminate the Taliban and to destroy Al Qaeda, and the military planners determined that the Special Operations Command Central (SOCCENT) would play a major role; the fight in Afghanistan would not be a conventional effort, so unconventional warfare would need to be emphasized. In the weeks following 9/11, Joint Special Operating Task Forces (JSOTFs) were designated for strategic deployment in the region, and each had been given their marching orders. In conjunction with Special Forces units from the 5th Special Forces Group, Madigan and his 10th SFGA ODA were to be deployed to Uzbekistan with the mission to help organize, train, equip and support the Afghan Northern Alliance Forces in the upcoming fight against Al Qaeda and the Taliban.

Madigan and his team arrived at Karshi-Khanabad Air Base in southeastern Uzbekistan in late September; this was to be their home and base of operations for the next 4 months. The following several weeks were feverish, working around the clock to get their Northern Alliance counterparts properly equipped and trained to work in smooth harmony with the ODA members. Meanwhile, massive air strikes into enemy strongholds inside Afghanistan began on October 7th and continued for most of the next two weeks. Once it was judged that the air war had inflicted sufficient damage upon the enemy, Northern Alliance forces, both in vehicles and on horseback, began to cross the border and move into Afghanistan; there they would be joined by SF operational detachments to conduct the next phase of the effort to eliminate the terrorists.

In late October, Madigan's ODA was airlifted into Afghanistan in the early morning hours on their UH-60 Blackhawk helicopter to the designated landing zone near Mazar-e-Sharif; there they linked up with Northern Alliance Forces under the command of General Abdul Rashid Dostum, a warlord with a strong power base in this area. Being denied any close combat role by General Dostum, the ODA members broke up into smaller 2-man teams, on horseback, to accompany Dostum's units for the upcoming assault on Mazar-e-Sharif; their role was to establish observation posts (OP) from where they could monitor the fight and call in close air support on enemy positions. This proved to be a lethal partnership, which inflicted significant damage to the enemy, both physically and psychologically, in their attempts to defend the city. During the final phases of this assault, Captain Madigan and his commo sergeant manned an OP overlooking the city of Mazar-e-Sharif; while

Madigan was calling in air support for the battle at hand, a Taliban soldier, armed with a Soviet-made RPG, had spotted the enemy in the OP and fired upon them. Madigan's commo sergeant saw the rocket trail headed towards them, but his warning came too late.

The rocket made a direct hit close to the commo sergeant and he was instantly obliterated by the blast; Madigan was a few feet away, and was partly protected from the blast by his comrade, but he was also badly hit by shrapnel. The first conscious thought which came to Madigan was ethereal, as he seemed to be floating above the spot where his buddy used to be as well as his own badly-wounded body; he was shocked to find himself looking down upon his inert physical self, seemingly lifeless, bloody, and badly wounded although Madigan believed that he must still be alive. He could also see a small group of his Afghan and ODA comrades racing their horses towards his OP position, obviously responding to the blast. Once they reached the spot where the OP had been, the ODA medic spotted Madigan and jumped from his horse to give medical attention. At that point, Madigan seemed to float away, higher and higher from his body, until he came to a place of brilliant light and vibrant color, such as he had never seen before.

Madigan was astounded by the pure beauty and peace of that which surrounded him. There was no understanding of what he was experiencing, just an overwhelming recognition of perfection, of absolute calm and astute consciousness. If this was heaven, it was nothing like the nuns had ever described for him; this was simply beyond description. Madigan's attention was then drawn to what he believed was another being appearing before him; to his amazement, this being began to assume the shape and appearance of what family pictures reflected as his father, Patrick. This was confirmed to Madigan when the spiritual being began to communicate with him, thoughts of loving guidance as a father would have for his son. Yet, although much of importance was communicated between them, the recollection of time spent was fleeting before Madigan found himself being torn from this place of perfection back to the previous existence he had just so abruptly departed.

Chapter III:

By the time Ksenia moved to Atotsi to assume her teaching position, it was 1942 and the world was aflame with the horrors of global conflict. No more than 2,000 people lived in the small rural town of Atotsi; nevertheless, many of the sons of Atotsi, and those from other nearby villages, had volunteered for the Soviet Army in 1941 to defend their homeland from the German invaders.

Ksenia was teaching accounting and mathematics to high school age students, and loved her work as a teacher; she was by nature a giving, service-oriented person, and it thrilled her to witness her students grow in knowledge. Her warm, personable demeanor also made her a favorite with her students, and their families, and she quickly acclimated herself within her new chosen community. One of her most enthusiastic students was young Kolya Donauri, an engaging young man of 15, whose family had taken a special liking to Ksenia, and who would frequently invite her to their small farm for family activities and dinner.

Based on her younger years in Lopani, Ksenia was always fascinated by how much self-sufficiency could be accomplished on a small family farm. Like her own family, the Donauri family had a thriving enterprise that provided most of the agricultural products they ever would need to consume; they had cows, pigs, chickens, fruit trees, a well-tended vegetable garden, and they also maintained a few beehives to produce honey and beeswax from which to make their own candles. With electricity being frequently subject to extended outages, the candles they produced from their bees provided badly-needed lighting during the times when the electricity went down. Ksenia took a keen interest in the Donauri beekeeping operation, and Kolya, the family member responsible for the bees, took great satisfaction in showing off his extensive knowledge to her.

It was also during this time that Ksenia first learned of Kolya's older cousin, Gurgena, who was one of the young men of Georgia who had answered the call to defend the homeland against the Nazi invasion. Gurgena lived in the nearby village of Gomi; immediately after graduation from high school on June 21st, 1942, Gurgena, along with several of his friends, had volunteered for the Soviet Army. Following a brief basic training period in the early fall of 1942, Gurgena had been assigned to the North Caucasian Front, under the command of Field Marshall Semyon Budenny. The German invasion of the Caucasus Region was well underway; the German's ultimate goal was to capture the strategically important oil fields located in Azerbaijan. The southern elements of the Nazi invasion force skirted the Caucasian Mountains, from where Soviet detachments, including Gurgena's unit, engaged the Germans in guerilla-type encounters intended to impede the invasion effort.

In the early winter of 1942, while positioning themselves for an attack on German forces near the Abkhazian border with Russia, Gurgena's unit was moving through a mountain pass in the Kodori Gorge region; following a period of very heavy snowfall, they were hit by a sudden avalanche, which buried many soldiers unable to find proper cover. One of the affected Soviet soldiers was Gurgena Donauri; he was fortunate to find some cover under a rock outcropping before the avalanche hit in full force. Although Gurgena was mostly covered by the snow and debris from the avalanche, especially the lower half of his body, he did fortunately have some airspace in which to breathe and, hopefully, to await rescue.

For most of the next 24 hours, in terribly frigid weather, the unaffected soldiers tried desperately to rescue their comrades; many were saved, and eventually survived, but survival, for the most part, came with a cost. In Gurgena's case, having spent about 16 hours trying to survive while waiting for his comrades to rescue him, all of his toes were so severely frostbitten that, after his liberation from his wintry prison, his toes needed to be amputated. Gurgena remained in hospital rehabilitation and therapy to try to learn to walk again for the following three months, after which he was medically discharged from the Soviet Army; thus, in March of 1943, he returned to his family home in Gomi to try to pick up his life again.

Ksenia had heard of Gurgena, and of his service and injuries in the Soviet Army, from her visits to the Donauri farm. Not too long after his return to Gomi, Gurgena joined his uncle, aunt and cousins at their farm in Atotsi for a Sunday dinner; as often happened, Ksenia had also been invited to join the Donauri family, an event at which she finally had the opportunity to meet Gurgena in person. It was love at first sight.

Gurgena was a rugged-looking, but handsome young man, blessed with a very gregarious personality; being more on the quiet and reflective side, Ksenia truly appreciated Gurgena's ability to preside over family court and be the center of attention while engaging all present in lively conversation.

Perhaps most impressive to Ksenia was Gurgena's tremendously positive outlook on life, especially having lost all of his toes and struggling to learn to walk again. None of the realities which World War II had bestowed upon him seemed to dim his joie de vivre and mental energy. Ksenia was drawn to him as metal to a magnet, and this became quite clear to the Donauri family from the outset; based on their extreme affection for Ksenia, it made for a perfect potential outcome for their beloved nephew and cousin, Gurgena.

With this happy development, Ksenia became a more frequent guest to the Donauri farm; although she had already come to be considered as a new member of the family prior to Gurgena's return from service, the mutual attraction that instantly developed between the two sealed the deal. Ksenia found herself visiting the Donauri family quite often, and, not coincidentally, Gurgena would also make the trip from Gomi to join the festivities. Not only did Ksenia greatly enjoy his company, but she also found joy in helping Gurgena through his challenging rehabilitation; even when he would often stumble or fall, Ksenia's heart would be melted by his instant rebound to the task at hand, and his unwaveringly positive attitude to make the best of his difficult situation. Gurgena never displayed any sign of self-pity; the only time he would display any sadness was when discussing his fallen comrades, who had not been as fortunate as Gurgena.

Gurgena's one concern in his budding relationship with Ksenia, as well as with his new life in general, was whether or not, in light of his disability, he would be able to get a job and to develop the means to support a family. He had always been technically-oriented, and had often helped out around the house with making repairs for household needs;

but he was now worried that he might find himself unable to walk, balance himself or move normally in response to work requirements. Although his interest in Ksenia as a possible wife was enormous, he lacked the confidence in his potential as a bread-winner and was therefore reluctant to make a proposal of marriage. Finally, after about two years of courtship, several realities developed which convinced him to take the step; firstly, he had sufficiently managed to overcome his disability to the point where he walked and maintained his balance with near normality, and, secondly, in the late spring of 1945, World War II finally came to end.

After much anxiety and concern from the standpoint of Ksenia and the entire Donauri family, it was in the autumn of 1945 when Gurgena finally proposed marriage to Ksenia, a proposal that she immediately and joyously accepted. With the war having come to an end, and the USSR having been depleted of massive human and financial resources by so many years of warfare, the general economic conditions and infrastructure of the Soviet Union, including the Republic of Georgia, were in poor condition. As a result, although they loved life in rural Georgia, Gurgena and Ksenia decided that their best prospects for the economic stability required to live comfortably and to raise a family were probably in a larger city. So, once they were married in the late spring of 1946, they left their beloved village life and moved to the capitol of Tbilisi, where Ksenia's family still lived.

Upon settling in Tbilisi, with the help of her parents, the newly-married couple settled into a small apartment in Tbilisi. Ksenia was able to identify a position as an accountant fairly quickly, and, after a couple of months, mostly due to his father-in-law's influence within the local Communist Party,

Gurgena was also able to obtain a position as a warehouse employee at the city jail. Between them, they earned enough money to live in a reasonably comfortable lifestyle, and, despite the inherent economic and social difficulties of living in post-war Soviet Union, Ksenia and Gurgena were happy and optimistic about the future. It did not take long before Ksenia became pregnant with their first child, and a son, David, was born in 1947; a second son, Adam, arrived two years later. With a rapidly growing family, space in their small apartment quickly became insufficient, but they were fortunate to find a small, older house on a larger lot that they could afford to purchase; the building required significant repair before the cold weather came upon them, but Gurgena and a few comrades were able to get the home into decent condition before winter. Life for the happy young family was good.

As their two boys grew over the coming years, Gurgena managed to build a couple of extensions onto the house; these were used for additional space for their family, but the entrepreneurially-minded Ksenia also was able to rent out one bedroom to university students to provide additional income. There was sufficient land on their plot to plant and tend a vegetable garden, as well as to plant a few fruit trees, all of which helped to supplement their needs during difficult times. Politically, this was still during the reign of Josef Stalin, so that life in Georgia was never predictably stable; in the early 1950's, Gurgena's family in Gomi came under some unfortunate political scrutiny due to perceived "illegal capitalistic practices," which led to both his father and uncle being incarcerated in the gulag for an extended period of time. Luckily, their imprisonment did not seem to have any immediate blowback upon Gurgena, probably again due to the influence that his father-in-law, Giorgi, had accumulated through years of faithful Communist Party service.

The later 1950's following the death of Stalin, and the 1960's, witnessed a growing sense of peace, stability and contentment for Ksenia, Gurgena and their two sons. Both boys were excellent students, and they were admitted in the mid-to-late 1960's to the State Technical University in Tbilisi, where they continued to excel; both graduated with degrees in mechanical engineering, David in 1968 and Adam in 1970. The two boys also had required mandatory military service obligations to uphold, but, whereas the Cold War was in full swing, there were no real hotspots of military conflict, and neither boy faced any major danger while fulfilling their active duty requirements. Later, with their military obligations behind them, and due to the fact that Tbilisi was a major manufacturing center for the USSR, both young men were able to find good engineering positions; and, in keeping with traditional life in Georgia, both also met suitable young ladies with whom to start their own family lives.

With the boys having completed their university studies, and off on the path of building their own lives, Gurgena and Ksenia, nostalgic for the quiet and tranquil lifestyle of the village, decided to sell their house in Tbilisi and to move to Gomi; Gurgena's childhood home there had been vacated by the death of his parents in the late 1960's, and he and Ksenia had used it as a "dacha" (country house) during the last years they lived in Tbilisi. Of course, moving from Tbilisi would mean leaving their jobs and the relative economic security that they had come to appreciate; however, with the funds they had accrued with the sale of their house in Tbilisi, their inherent work ethic and Ksenia's entrepreneurial spirit, they were confident that they could enjoy a comfortable and gratifying life back in the rural Georgian environment that they both loved.

Similar to Ksenia's previous village experiences in Lopani and Atotsi, Gomi was a small rural village where a few thousand people resided; however, Gomi was much more "on the beaten track" than the other two villages with a major east-west highway, as well as a stop on the train route, running between Tbilisi and Batumi on the Black Sea coast. The Donauri home, like that of Ksenia's family in Lopani and the Donauri cousins in Atotsi, was a smaller home built upon a reasonably large plot of land, nearly a hectare in size. Gurgena's grandparents had been the first occupants of the home beginning in the 1870's, and three generations of utilizing the land to its fullest advantage was clearly evident. After moving into the house on a permanent basis in 1972, Ksenia and Gurgena put their own unique mark on the property.

The plot of land surrounding the home featured an abundance of fruit trees which provided a bountiful harvest every year; these included golden and red apple trees, black and yellow cherry trees, and numerous plum, pear and walnut trees. All of these gave birth to food products that would be integrated into their traditional Georgian cuisine each year.

The vegetable garden was also quite comprehensive, sufficient for Georgian culinary practices, containing red beans, white potatoes, tomatoes, green and red peppers, and sweet corn, in addition to essential herbs such as parsley and cilantro. Livestock on the farmette was a bit more limited, but provided most of the dietary essentials; Ksenia always had 1-2 cows to provide milk and cheese products, a few pigs for meat products and a couple of dozen chickens for fresh eggs and poultry meat.

The most visible crop in evidence on the property, however, was the impressively lengthy line of grape vines which bordered and covered the 100-meter-long driveway entering the property; driving to the house, one was surrounded by vines on both sides and overhead (hanging from the grape trellis) with an abundance of red and white grapes from which the harvest that provided the family's own wine supply would be made.

Every year in mid-to-late October, just before the weather began to turn wintry cold, Ksenia would gather the family at their home for the annual grape harvest and wine-making festivities. The harvest of the grapes constituted an annual family activity which required several days of intensive labor but which was also considered family fun. The white "Odessa" grapes, a regional varietal which produced a dry wine similar to a Sauvignon Blanc and which constituted the majority of the crop, would be harvested first; this would be followed by the harvest of the "Dirbula" vines, another popular regional grape, which produces a red wine that is semi-sweet in flavor, somewhat similar to a Pinot Noir.

The cutting of the grape bunches was handled by the more experienced members of the family, while the carting of the grapes and operation of the crusher could be relegated to the younger generation. The crusher was a relatively simple device with a funnel for the loading of the grape bunches, a hand-operated crushing device which would process the bunches of grapes and press out the juice, all of which would be emptied into a collection trough; in the trough, the juice would be processed and emptied via a tubing system into

5-gallon canisters while the "pomace" (stems, skins and debris left from the crushing process) would be separated for subsequent use in the making of Cha-Cha, a Georgian grape vodka.

Once in the canister, the wine fermentation process, requiring a minimum of 8 – 9 months, would begin; the canisters would be stored in the dark, cool basement of the house which provided optimum conditions for the fermentation of the wine. During this time, a secondary filtering of the canisters, to extract any pomace which was not removed during the initial separation process, would take place after the first month and, if needed, during subsequent months. The wine would be suitable for consumption after this 8-9 month fermentation process (somewhere around June or July), although additional aging of the wine continued to improve the final product.

From Ksenia's small wine harvest, the family would normally produce about 400-450 liters of white wine, and, from the smaller harvest of the Dirbula grapes, another 60-75 liters of red wine. In addition, the secondary processing of the grape pomace, to which water was added to be boiled together in a large stainless steel pot, from which the vodka-like "Cha-Cha" was produced, yielded about 40 liters of this very potent product.

Once ready for consumption, the wine would be divided among the family, and would provide excellent wine for the coming year, until the following year's harvest would be ready to consume. The wine also provided the opportunity for competition between other family members and friends to determine who had produced the highest quality wine during the year's harvest, a great source of annual bragging rights and pride.

The very high level of self-sufficiency derived from their farmette was very gratifying to Ksenia; however, her most favorite undertaking was her own beekeeping operation which she introduced soon after moving to Gomi.

Chapter IV:

Madigan finally awoke at the American Regional Medical Center in Landstuhl, Germany, next to the U.S. air base at Ramstein. It was almost two weeks following the attack on Mazar-e-Sharif during which he had been gravely wounded by an incoming RPG round. Although he had fallen from consciousness into a coma after being hit by the blast of the RPG, and having taken shrapnel to the head and chest, he was airlifted to a nearby military outpost where he had undergone emergency surgery to stem the tide of death; as soon as possible following the emergency surgery, he was then airlifted to Landstuhl, where several additional surgeries had transpired. Madigan finally regained consciousness there, but it required many additional days before he began to comprehend what miraculous events he had recently experienced.

For Ryan, after two weeks of being comatose, he endeavored to come to terms with the reality of his physical injuries. Although he had taken shrapnel to his head, which had contributed the most to his loss of consciousness, he was extremely fortunate that it had not penetrated his brain too deeply; as luck would have it, that shrapnel which had reached the brain was easily removed at Landstuhl without imparting permanent damage to his mental capacity. Several additional surgeries had transpired to remove shrapnel from his chest and torso area; there was serious damage to one of his lungs and related arterial damage, but, all in all, Madigan was judged highly fortunate to have survived. Naturally, much of his conscious thought was monopolized by feelings of severe grief for his comms sergeant who had been killed by the blast, as well as for the physical pain that he was suffering from the multiple surgeries; however, the most confounding aspect for him of the past two weeks had been the surreal episode following the blast of which he amazingly had total recall.

Ryan had totally remembered the spiritual, out-of-body experience to which he had been ethereally transported just two weeks ago, but it was simply beyond his capability to understand it, or to even believe that it might have actually happened to him. Having been raised a devout Roman Catholic, Madigan maintained a strong religious faith and belief in the hereafter, but the apparent out-of-body experience, and the encounter with the spirit of his father, was just too far outside of the boundaries of faith for him to fully accept. Nevertheless, it was constantly on his mind.

Lest he possibly be accused of having lost his sanity, Ryan decided to keep the matter of the spiritual encounter with his father entirely to himself. Although his army career may well be damaged by the extent of the serious physical injuries that he had suffered, he was certain that the Army would send him packing if he starting talking about having a friendly get-together with his Dad in Heaven. Yet, Madigan needed to find some answers for no other reason than his own sanity, so, once he was able gain partial mobility and to move around the hospital complex, he went straight to the hospital library where he started to research out-of-body, near death experiences. After several days of intensive research, he was still not entirely convinced that he had not completely lost his mind, but at least he had found enough pertinent information to corroborate the possibility that his experience might have been legitimate.

Since he had regained consciousness, Madigan had become quite popular with the doctors and nurses who called on him throughout the day while making their appointed rounds. Naturally, the fact that he had successfully come out of his coma made him an instant celebrity amongst the hospital staff, but moreover he was a handsome and engaging patient, who had quickly captured the affection of male and female attendants alike. Foremost among his circle of his new-found friends was First Lieutenant Kelly Cooper, a physician's assistant who was similar in age to Madigan, but with whom he had quickly developed a sense of trust and intellectual commonality. If there was one person here at Landstuhl with whom he could trust his secret experience, he felt confident that it was Kelly.

After a few weeks of recuperation from his injury-imposed surgeries, Ryan was allowed to be wheeled outside on the expansive and attractive hospital grounds for an occasional breath of fresh air. Since, on that day, the weather was beautiful and she had completed her daily rounds, Ryan was able to convince Lt. Cooper to escort him on an excursion down to the duck pond. Once they had arrived, they both settled down on a bench overlooking the pond, and, after sufficient small talk, Madigan decided to carefully broach the topic that had concerned him so deeply. He was prepared for the possibility that she might very well react negatively to his revelation, but he felt that he knew her well enough by this time, and that they had developed a sufficiently solid rapport, to take the risk. After finally accumulating enough courage to broach the matter of his near death experience, Ryan noticed that Kelly had assumed a deeply contemplative demeanor, and, after a minute of two of quiet reflection, he was highly relieved by her careful response.

Kelly told him that he was not the first soldier who had confided in her with such a revelation; there had been a similar case with a patient whom she attended just three months prior. She admitted to Madigan that she had initially been quite surprised and shocked by the previous soldier's disclosure, but that it had compelled her to research the topic as well; the information that she had found was that this was not an entirely unique experience, particularly with serious combat injuries, and that it had convinced her sufficiently not to discount the possibility. The details of her research that she shared with Ryan, and the convincing description of her former patient's experience, was enough to offer the idea to Madigan that he had not gone crazy after all. The sense of intense relief that he felt from this warm and compassionate conversation with Kelly was incredibly gratifying, and he immediately sensed the lifting of a burdensome millstone from his psyche. When it was time to return to his hospital room, they agreed to keep their conversation just between the two of them, at least for the time being; the ride in the wheelchair back to his room was blessed with mutually-contented silence, yet Madigan knew that his future life, from that point forward, would be remarkably changed by what he had experienced on that battlefield in Afghanistan.

*   *   *   *   *

Ryan and Kelly never discussed their pond-side conversation again, but their non-verbal exchanges henceforth revealed a true sense of mutual understanding. It was clear to Madigan that she believed him totally, and that she would keep her promise not to reveal his personal disclosure. After another six weeks of continued treatment for his injuries and physical therapy, Madigan received orders that he would be sent back to Ft. Carson to rejoin the 10th Special Forces Group, from where future career decisions would be made; however, the incredibly impactful spiritual exchange that he had experienced with his father had already convinced Ryan where his future life's path might lead him.

The message from his father, Patrick, who had lost his life in combat in southeast Asia when Ryan was still an infant, was clear and concise. It was not Ryan's destiny, his father had said, to die on the battlefield as he had done, but rather to live a full and fruitful life in other, more spiritual pursuits. His father had decried the extreme loss and pain that his own early death had caused his wife, Mary Ellen, and that Ryan should not burden his mother with further such pursuits. Patrick had confided the message that the right path for Ryan in his coming years would always be mentally clear to him, and that he had much still to contribute during his lifetime. Patrick had concluded their spiritual conversation with the guidance that Ryan's heart, the wisdom drawn from spiritual sources, would always serve him well, and he should trust those instincts completely; Patrick had added that he would always be omnipresent, within Ryan's intuitive consciousness, to help to guide him forward.

It was March of 2002 when Ryan was finally released from the hospital in Landstuhl for his return to Fort Carson. The afternoon prior to his release was highlighted by a small but heartfelt farewell celebration with the hospital staff for whom Ryan was so deeply grateful; this included a warm and long embrace with Lieutenant Cooper, with whom Ryan had felt such a special connection. In fact, Ryan and Kelly would continue communications following his departure, never again broaching the topic of their secret conversation, yet confident in the knowledge that theirs was a special, purposeful bond, blessed by a rare and spiritually intimate mutual trust.

Upon arrival at Fort Carson, Captain Madigan was assigned to the Headquarters element of the 10th SFGA, in an administrative capacity. This was not an uncommon occurrence for soldiers who had experienced serious battlefield trauma; furthermore, since Madigan had less than one year remaining on his current commitment, it would provide a less stressful assignment during which Madigan could decide upon his future career path. Having received the guidance from his father loud and clear, and not having any doubt about the content, Madigan was still badly conflicted with the prospect of leaving the U.S. Army; he loved what he did, and took great pride in representing his country, but he certainly did not want to ignore the guidance from his father, particularly the plea to consider his mother when making future decisions. So, when Ryan took two weeks leave to spend some time with his mother in early May of 2002, this was the dilemma that he was facing.

After arriving at his mother's home in Chevy Chase, and spending just one day there, he drove down to Ocean City, Maryland, with his mother, where she had a beach house; the summer renters would soon occupy the house until Labor Day, but it was available for Ryan and Mary Ellen to enjoy the beauty of the ocean and solitude during their sunrise walks together. This time at the beach, especially during their morning walks, offered Ryan and Mary Ellen the environment in which to discuss the events of the past year. Mary Ellen had flown to Germany to be with Ryan in the hospital, both while he was comatose and later, but that was no time for the discussion of serious topics; his mother had simply been grateful that he had survived his serious injuries. But, although Ryan had mentioned to his mother the inclination that he might leave the Army, he stopped short of revealing his spiritual conversation with his father, for fear that this might simply be too much for her to handle. Perhaps it was better to save that revelation for some other, more appropriate, time, if there could ever be one.

After returning from the beach house to Chevy Chase, Ryan still had a few days before he needed to return to Fort Carson, so, under the "cover" of a pleasure drive in the Blue Ridge mountains, he set off on a personal mini-mission that he had planted in his mind to accomplish at the first opportunity. During his post-comatose time in Landstuhl, he had discovered in the hospital library a fascinating book covering the topic of out-of-body experiences, written by Robert Monroe in 1971; Monroe had since founded The Monroe Institute in the foothills of the Blue Ridge in Virginia for the exploration of, and training in, various spiritual and psychic phenomena. Since reading Monroe's book, he had felt a strong intuitive need to visit the Institute, and this seemed like the perfect opportunity.

Upon arriving at Monroe Institute, Ryan felt an immediate sense of increased energy surrounding him, like a welcoming, loving embrace from someone dear. He began to feel that he had been intentionally drawn to this place for some specific reason, one which might even possibly enable him to come to terms with his future life's path. He did not know what, if any, impact this visit might have, but he did feel a sort of certainty that he was meant to be here.

Following the near death, out-of-body encounter he had with his late father resulting from the battlefield in Afghanistan, Ryan had also recalled what he believed were similar out-of-body experiences while in a dreamlike state. One of these happened while he was still comatose in the Landstuhl hospital; he had found himself hovering over his body in the hospital room, with his mother beside his body, weeping forlornly and praying that her beloved son would return to her. He remembered his feeling of frustration that he could not reach out to her, to comfort her, and tell her that he was there with her, and that he would return to her soon. One or two similar dreams were vaguely in his memory, unclear in specific content, but real enough to convince him that he might find the answers here, in this special place in the foothills of the Blue Ridge, which Robert Monroe had purposely selected as the location for his Institute.

It was during this visit that Ryan met several persons with whom he hoped to have future contact. One was an elderly gentleman who taught the Monroe Institute's intensive course on out-of-body (OBE) experiences and another was a middle-aged gentleman and Army veteran, who, during his active duty days, had become an expert in the little known psychic phenomenon of Remote Viewing; this is the ability to envision remote locations while in a psychic state and to depict those locations to colleagues controlling the process. Ryan had felt sufficiently comfortable with both of these gentlemen to discuss his OBE recollections with them; both men had listened attentively, and had encouraged Ryan to consider returning to the Institute to undergo one of their week-long courses in out-of-body experiences. Ryan departed the Institute later that afternoon with the feeling that he had been exposed to something that he would surely wish to experience, in the hope that he might find some future validation to the otherwise inexplicable recollections of his out-of-body experiences.

On the return drive to Chevy Chase that evening, Madigan began to feel that he had truly come upon a resource that would help him to put into context why he had been chosen to return to life with the knowledge that experiences beyond the physical form existed. He still did not know how he could make good use of these psychic phenomena, but he was clear in his own mind that he needed to investigate these unique experiences to a much greater extent. Whereas he decided that he would certainly take full advantage of this opportunity at some future date, he realized that he still had some important decisions to make vis-à-vis his near-term career path.

After a few more pleasant, but emotional, days in Chevy Chase with his mother, Madigan flew back to resume his assignment at Fort Carson, to the Special Forces unit that he loved; however, he did so with the realization that destiny had other future pursuits planned for him in the years to come.

Chapter V:

With the move having been made from Tbilisi to Gomi in the summer of 1972, and with their two sons off beginning lives of their own, Ksenia found herself with the need to replace the income that she and Gurgena had earned from their jobs in Tbilisi. To put their situation into historical perspective, the late 1960's and early 1970's were years of poor economic development and growth in the USSR under the leadership (or lack thereof) of General Secretary Leonid Brezhnev. It was a period when families were struggling to support themselves throughout the USSR. For Ksenia, the solution presented itself in the early fall of 1972 when she and Gurgena went to the village of Atotsi to visit his cousin, Kolya; a recent telephone conversation with Kolya, from whom she had initially learned about beekeeping many years before, had reminded her of a past idea.

In order to earn supplemental income in those days of government ownership of all official business enterprises, Kolya had supplemented his income by raising bees, and producing honey and beeswax; Vladimir Lenin, in 1919, had judged that the raising of bees could have positive environmental and agricultural effects, and he had passed a law that would exclude revenue from beekeeping from taxation. Although he only had 5 beehives, Kolya mentioned to Ksenia that, per harvest from each hive, he could produce 20-30 kilograms of honey and a 1-2 kilograms of beeswax, from which he could generate a reasonable second income. Having piqued her interest by showing her the basics of beekeeping and by touting the money that could potentially be made, Ksenia quizzed Kolya mercilessly during their week-long visit; by the time that she and Gurgena started their return trip to Gomi, Ksenia had already mentally developed her plan of action for starting and building a beekeeping business at their home.

During the winter of 1972-73, Ksenia read everything she could on beekeeping, the equipment she would need and how to successfully begin a bee colony. Like cousin Kolya, she started her beekeeping venture that Spring with 5 hives at her home in Gomi. During that initial season, she used the basic education from what she had researched and learned from Kolya, and she completed that first year with a good production from two harvests, one in the late spring and the second in the late summer.

Ksenia had also learned that in order to produce a unique and distinctive flavor to her honey production, it is best to vary the locations of the hives at least once per harvest, thus allowing the bees to produce honey from different varieties of flowers. During that following spring of 1974, Ksenia started her bees in her village area, and then transported them in the mid- spring to an area where her good childhood friend Natia lived; this was in the village of Didi Plevi, where different flower varieties prospered, about sixty kilometers west of Gomi. There one could find plentiful patches of acacia trees, which flowered prolifically and were a magnet for the bee colony. Honey with acacia added to the hive creates a product that possesses a mild, sweet and floral flavor that is also quite clear in appearance and also slow to crystallize. Ksenia was so pleased with her initial production that she used the same routine and returned there again later that summer for the second harvest.

In the years to come, each Spring, and again in the late Summer, Ksenia would stay with Natia in Plevi for several weeks at a time; the bees would flourish in the new setting, abounding with countless varieties of wild flowers and fruit trees in addition to the acacia. Per her estimates, honey production would increase significantly during these, as Ksenia used to describe them, "bee vacations." While the bees performed their magic in the new glens and valleys of Plevi, Ksenia and Natia would happily perform chores together, relive old times of their childhood together, and share their personal stories of life learned as an adult. Their friendship was such that their time together never grew old, as every new day brought forth stories to share and experiences to create.

The harvest of the bee's honey production would usually take place in early June and again, at summer's end, around early September. At the rate of production of 20-30 kilograms per harvest per hive, plus the ancillary 1-2 kilograms of beeswax production, Ksenia's 5 hives produced a significant harvest her first few years; at summer's end, with a total annual production of nearly 300 kilos of honey and 20 kilos of beeswax, she was able to earn quite a significant income for the household. In those days, honey sold for about 4 Soviet Rubles per liter, and beeswax, which was sold almost exclusively to the Georgian Orthodox churches, would bring about 3 Rubles per kilogram. Ksenia's network of friends and former colleagues from her years living and working in Tbilisi were eager to purchase her honey, and she quickly sold her beeswax production to a few of her favorite churches in Tbilisi. Accordingly, at the end of her first year of beekeeping, Ksenia earned about 1,200 Rubles from the endeavor, which was a significant contribution to the family's income.

Based on the success of her initial harvests, Ksenia reinvested her profits and expanded the number of her hives each and every year, to the point where she had eventually built a large enterprise. By the mid-1980's, she had 70 bee hives, which was one of the largest beekeeping operations in the entire country. During the gradual process of increasing the number of beehives on their small plot of land to as many as 70, the operation had quickly become too much for Ksenia to handle by herself. As she methodically increased the number of hives each year, Ksenia needed Gurgena's assistance more and more to manage the increased work requirements from the larger operation. In addition, the twice-annual bee vacations became a major logistical exercise, which required Gurgena full-time plus extra manpower on both ends of the trip, so additional part-time help needed to be hired as well. By the mid-1980's, with the 70 hives producing an average of about 4,000 kilograms of honey per year and about 300 kilograms of beeswax, Ksenia's beekeeping operation, despite increased production and sales costs, was netting them around 15,000 Rubles per year, which, at the time, was a tidy sum.

During Soviet times, despite the fact that beekeeping maintained a tax-free legal status in the USSR, it was never wise to showcase entrepreneurial success in the anti-capitalist state, so Ksenia and Gurgena maintained a low profile and did not advertise their financial windfall. Although they had needed to increase their visibility by selling much of their production in farmer's markets in various venues throughout the region, they still managed to maintain a relatively low visibility so that government predators never harassed them. However, the success of their beekeeping operation did allow Ksenia and Gurgena to travel to Moscow for 1-2 months every winter; there they would stay with friends, sell their honey and beeswax in the central market, and purchase products that were very hard to find in Tbilisi, particularly clothing and gifts for the family at home. All in all, life for them at this point in history was relatively affluent, at least by Soviet standards.

By the mid 1980's, news of her success as a beekeeper had become so widely known in pertinent agricultural circles that Kseniya was hired as a consultant by a large collective farm in the region of her village of Gomi; her job was to oversee their beekeeping operation and advise on how to increase and improve their production. Although the collective farm consulting position did not compensate Ksenia very much, it did much to enhance her reputation within Georgia, to the point where Ksenia became widely considered as one of the foremost experts on beekeeping in the country.

In 1992, Gurgena began to suffer some major health problems, which made it difficult for him to help Ksenia in the beekeeping business; by the next year, Gurgena was largely bedridden, and the size of her bee operation was simply too much for Ksenia to manage alone. As a result, they decided that they needed to downsize their operation to a more manageable level. Ksenia sold most of her hives and equipment to the collective farm where she served as a consultant, and reduced her own bee endeavor to about 20 hives; this reduced operation still produced a significant annual harvest of honey and beeswax and thus provided a lucrative source of income. Combined with the consulting salary that Ksenia was receiving from the collective farm, their beekeeping endeavor continued to support them well.

Much more was happening within the USSR during the late

1980's and early 1990's, however, which would have a major impact on how Georgians would be living their lives, then and in the future. Following the reign of Leonid Brezhnev as General Secretary of the CPSU, which ended in his death in 1983, he was succeeded by the brief, death-shortened regimes of Yuri Andropov and Konstantin Chernenko, neither of whom did anything to improve the stagnant economy and dissipating international power of the Soviet Union. The election of the reform-minded Mikhail Gorbachev as General Secretary in 1985 introduced the concepts of "Perestroika" (restructuring) and "Glasnost" (openness), which would make a huge impact on everyday life in the USSR, especially in the outlying Republics such as Georgia. Although the prevailing view of that period of history is debatable, the time of Gorbachev's rule led to the final death toll for the USSR, as it was officially dissolved in 1991.

Following the break-up of the Soviet Union, and Georgia's Declaration of Independence in April, 1991, a coup d'etat of the initial post-USSR Georgian government took place in December of that year, followed by a massive struggle between conflicting parties for the power to rule Georgia; unable to resolve the issues by political means, a Civil War broke out which created major havoc, especially in the cities, and lasted well into 1995. People who lived in the villages of Georgia, like Ksenia and Gurgena, who were largely self-sufficient as producers of foodstuffs and other products needed to survive, were better prepared to combat the shortfall of food during the civil war years. Ksenia had even purchased a nearby plot of vacant farmland where she planted wheat in order to produce flour and make bread since normal production sources had been disrupted by the civil war; in this way, Ksenia was able to produce enough flour and bread to ensure supply of her Gomi community of friends as well as her sons and their families in Tbilisi where food was especially scarce due to the disruption of production and distribution of food.

Although Ksenia managed to avoid most of the dangers and hardships imposed during the Civil War, and to survive relatively well, her beloved husband, Gurgena, sadly passed away at the age of 74 due to illness, shortly after the conclusion of the Civil War in 1995. Gurgena had not only been the "love of her life," but he had always been her best friend and closest confidant during their nearly 40 years of married life. Ksenia had herself turned 71 just prior to his death, and, with his passing, she felt a void, an emptiness in her life that she had never before experienced. But she had two sons who had never been absent in the lives of their parents, and 5 beloved grandchildren who were actively involved in the village life that Ksenia and Gurgena had so enjoyed together.

Since graduating from the University, Ksenia's two sons both were working full-time as successful engineers in different factories and began to raise families of their own; between them, they had given birth to 5 children between the years of 1977 and 1986, who had quickly become sources of great joy and beneficiaries of significant attention from their proud grandparents. As they grew in years and learned useful agricultural and culinary skills during their frequent visits to Gomi, Ksenia's grandchildren all became an important cog in the ever-spinning wheel of productivity at the farmette. Naturally, with both of her sons being successful mechanical engineers, Ksenia benefitted from the most creative and up-to-date technological advances of anyone in Gomi; added to that omnipresent advantage, the 5 grandchildren were all diligent and energetic practitioners of the multiple production processes that were always in motion at the farmette.

As their age and capabilities grew, all of the grandchildren had specific roles to play in a wide variety of chores that Ksenia made into entertaining and important missions to which the children responded enthusiastically. They engaged in milking and cleaning up after the cows, feeding the pigs and chickens, collecting the just-laid eggs, harvesting fruit, nuts or vegetables, and then helping to prepare the plethora of delicious dishes to be made from them. They also assumed active roles in Ksenia's beekeeping and winemaking operations, which were the most enjoyable of all, since these were the raison d'etre for large and joyous collective family gatherings.

Truth be told, Ksenia and Gurgena openly loved all of their grandchildren equally and never demonstrated any overt preference for any of them. They were all intelligent, respectful, well-raised and resourceful children of whom any parent or grandparent would be duly proud. However, Ksenia had especially seen the hand of God at work in the person of her middle grandchild, Tamara, who, with her loving disposition and her evident creative and problem-solving capabilities, seemed to be an absolute clone of Ksenia herself. Gurgena had been the first to bring this close resemblance to Ksenia's attention. Initially, she refused to acknowledge the close similarity, until, as years passed, the reality simply became undeniable. Ksenia and Tamara were clearly cut from the same cloth; although she tried her best not to betray her special fondness for her, Ksenia would often catch Gurgena's wide and knowing smile when he caught his wife's obvious admiration for her seemingly-cloned grandchild.

Anyone who witnessed the family collective at work or play together saw that the mutual admiration and genuine affection between the grandchildren and their grandparents was equally omnipresent. At the time of Gurgena's death, the grandchildren were between the ages of 9 to 19, and they manifested the sadness of his passing into love, empathy and support for their grieving grandmother. Tamara, in particular, paid especially close attention to Ksenia during the months following Gurgena's funeral, as if she understood inherently what Ksenia was feeling and what she needed in order to heal her grief. If it had not been quite as clear before that sad event, the bond that developed between them became fully welded with the strongest spiritual and emotional strength; this bond was never weakened between them, either by lengthy absences or the vast distances between them that Fate would eventually introduce.

Chapter VI:

Madigan returned to Ft. Carson following his two-week leave with his mother feeling physically and mentally refreshed, but with important, still unresolved, decisions to be made. Although he had another 10 months left on his current military commitment, he knew in his heart that he had already made his decision to leave the Army; but, what was to come next remained an issue that he still needed to resolve. However, he had developed a strong intuitive sense that his destiny would play out in its own time, so he was not worried that everything would eventually fall into place. He did know that he needed to announce his official decision soon that he would be leaving the service, but, except in his own mind, there was no real rush to do so.

In the months to follow, Ryan often mentally reviewed the impactful events of the past year, and became more strongly convinced that destiny had indeed chosen other paths for him to pursue. He was convinced that he wanted to further explore his brief insights into the spiritual realm, and that he wished to delve more deeply into the essence of his near death, out of body experiences; he was also confident that the Monroe Institute offered him one intriguing avenue in which to do so. As his father had urged him to do, Ryan knew that he needed to trust his instincts, to follow his heart and to understand how his pragmatic mind might offer counter arguments to the spiritual path. After all, despite the personal trauma he had faced during his service time, he had loved his Army Special Forces experience, but he understood that it was time to move on.

Ryan submitted his paperwork to leave the Army in September, 2002, and he was honorably discharged in March, 2003, after which he left Ft. Carson to return home to Chevy Chase. Madigan arrived home with his future plans still uncertain; however, he had already registered for a course at the Monroe Institute, which was slated to begin in April. In addition, he had received an email from an SF officer buddy whom he had met during the Q Course, and who had heard Ryan was leaving the Army; he said that he had a job opening for which Ryan was perfect that might possibly interest him.

During his visit to the Monroe Institute the previous spring, Ryan had learned that they offered intensive week-long courses on Near Death and Out of Body Experiences. Although Madigan had become reasonably comfortable with the fact of his own experiences within this realm, he definitely wanted to learn more from experts in this field, so he signed up for the first available offering; the course was to start within several weeks following his separation from the Army. When the day came on which the course was due to start, his mother asked Ryan where he was going; he still did not feel ready to discuss his OBE phenomenon with her, so he told her the white lie that he was going to visit friends, to play some golf and relax. Ryan did not like the fact that he had lied to his mother about his trip, but he hoped that this course might actually answer enough of his questions to enable him to share this secret part of his life upon his return home.

Following the legacy of its founder, the Monroe Institute had put together an intriguing, intensive live-in course on learning about, and potentially experiencing, out of body episodes. The instructor was a PhD with long personal experience on the subject matter, and the 20 or so students who had signed up for the course had one significant thing in common; they had all personally had near death, and/or out of body experiences in the past, and they all thirsted for much more knowledge. So, once the group had gathered for the first time, during which the instructor gave an overview of what to expect and all of the students had introduced themselves and shared why they had enrolled for the course, Ryan shed a few tears of emotion with the knowledge that he had indeed been beckoned wisely.

At the Monroe Institute, Madigan felt like he was in exactly the right place, at the precisely intended time, to be able to reconcile the issue of his near death experience and the inexplicable spiritual meeting with his father. Happily, he was surrounded by serious, empathetic people who were all on a similar quest; the other course participants were all looking for answers to mystical questions, just like he was. Throughout the week, Madigan often found himself feeling an overwhelming sense of gratitude for having been led to this perfectly-timed and pertinent destination. Each time that he felt this way, he would offer a brief prayer of thanks to his father.

The course participants concentrated on reaching heightened states of consciousness through intensive proprietary techniques that enabled most, if not all, of them to experience intentionally induced out of body realities and to return from the experience safely. Ryan was able to experience two additional out-of-body experiences during the course; although these were still a bit shocking to him, these OBE's provided him with the final assurances that his spiritual encounter with his father had been real. What Ryan found most surprising was the realization that one could, having reached a proper meditative state, actually initiate an out-of-body experience by choice; moreover, having meditated upon the precise purpose of the induced OBE, one could actually transport spiritually to a predetermined location for a chosen purpose. Ryan found this phenomenon to be mindboggling, yet it further provided comfort that his own experiences had not been a product of his imagination.

The course also developed a much fuller understanding of, and appreciation for, the psychic realm in which our spiritual guides readily interact with us during our physical manifestation, and provide us guidance which we normally consider simply intuitive. Finally, like Ryan, everyone who took part in the course came away with a genuine sense of relief and a far better understanding of what we humans will encounter after our life has come to an end. The ever-present millstone of the fear of death had been collectively lifted from an entire group of folks; they would now have the ability to more fully enjoy the blessings that life provided and make the most of every single moment made available to them on earth.

Shortly after returning to Chevy Chase, Ryan called his former SF colleague about the job opening of which he had been recently informed. Just one year prior, the U.S. Government had kicked off the Georgia Train and Equip Program (GTEP) with the former Soviet Republic, and Ryan's buddy had been among the first detachment of active duty Special Forces soldiers to be assigned to the program; they had been sent to train several brigades of Georgian soldiers to prepare them for eventual assignment to Afghanistan. Parallel to the GTEP, the USG was also beginning to mount another program, to be awarded to a Major American Defense Contracting company, that would require experienced former military personnel to perform assorted projects within the Georgian Ministry of Defense. One of these upcoming projects required a battle-proven former Special Operations Officer to be attached to the Georgian Special Forces Brigade for training and advisory purposes. The job carried only a one-year commitment, with no additional strings attached; it would enable Madigan to continue to work in his chosen field, without, hopefully at least, breaking his commitment to his father not to place his life at risk again.

Ryan promptly applied for the job opening, went soon thereafter for an interview in nearby Northern Virginia, and was offered the position quickly. If he were to accept, Ryan would be expected to deploy to Georgia in the next few weeks along with the initial group of contractors who would be servicing projects within the MOD. Ryan especially liked the freedoms he expected to have in this project; the ability to choose where he served, flexibility in the duration of service, the ability to create and manage (without an overbearing chain of command) a program to his liking, and to live a civilian-style lifestyle while still serving the nation. Since he had been to Georgia previously, during a brief familiarization mission in 1997, Ryan had developed a very positive impression for the beauty of the country and the extreme hospitality of the people; it all promised to be an exciting and enjoyable experience, and Ryan was ebullient when he departed from Dulles International Airport bound for Tbilisi in June of 2003.

Ryan's flight plan to Tbilisi transited Istanbul, where he boarded an afternoon Turkish Airways flight for the two-hour journey over the Black Sea and the length of Georgia. Even though it was early June, Ryan could see the massive Caucasus Mountain range in all of its snow-capped majesty from his window seat, and he was reminded again of the awe-inspiring natural beauty of the country. After landing and being met at Tbilisi International Airport, Ryan was taken by van to the Sheraton Metechi Palace Hotel overlooking Tbilisi. While viewing the city from his room balcony, he was once again highly impressed by the beauty and antiquity of the architecture in front of him; with a massive ancient stone fortress off to one side, and a myriad of historic churches and distinctive buildings dominating his view, the excitement he felt at that moment was palpable. He was suddenly overcome with the intuitive feeling that this magical place would somehow play a vitally important role in his ultimate destiny.

The first day in Tbilisi was a busy one. Initially he had a team meeting with the contractor group that had been assembled to work on the various projects with the Ministry, followed by an introduction to the Minister of Defense and his welcome to the American team. Following a group lunch with the Minister, Ryan was introduced to the Georgian interpreter who had been assigned as his assistant; her name was Nana, and Ryan was immediately impressed with her. Nana demonstrated absolute command of the English language which would prove indispensable to Ryan's ability to perform his job, plus she was a charming young Georgian lady with whom he believed he could develop a solid working relationship. Later that afternoon, Ryan and Nana set off to meet with Colonel Dolidze, commander of the Georgian Special Forces Brigade, whose given name was Roin, meaning "King." Roin was a wiry soldier of similar age, and Ryan felt that he was aptly named for the role that he played in his military assignment; he possessed inherent confidence and a command presence in his demeanor, and Ryan knew from the outset that he would be an excellent counterpart for the work ahead.

Over the weeks to come, Ryan worked closely with Colonel Dolidze to establish their project objectives, during which time he was also able to meet the other officers and men who composed the "misnamed" Special Forces Brigade. He considered it misnamed since the Special Forces contingent was much smaller than official Brigade strength; nevertheless, the unit was still comprised of experienced, competent Special Operators who were the cream of the crop among the Georgian Army forces. Whereas Madigan played the role of observer during those first few weeks, primarily measuring the capabilities of the Georgian SF operators, he was impressed by what he saw. These were top-notch soldiers, motivated to learn the modus operandi of their American colleagues, and to tackle whatever missions they might be called upon to conduct in the years ahead.

Following a two-week long training exercise in the high mountains of the Shatili region, the SF troops returned to Tbilisi, where, that Saturday, the Georgian Army Chief of Staff had planned a "supra" in honor of the American contractor team. The supra was held in a forested park in the ancient city of Mtskheta, where several famous Georgian Kings were buried in the city cathedral. Prior to the feast, while the Georgian officers diligently prepared the meal, the American team was given a tour of Mtskheta, the cathedral and the several historical museums and archeological sites in the city center. It was there and then, during the tour of this ancient city, that Madigan was struck by Cupid's arrow.

One of the volunteer tour leaders was a stunning young brunette, who immediately caught Madigan's attention. She was tall and statuesque, but it was her ready smile and contagious laugh that mesmerized Ryan. He spent the first hour of the tour simply admiring her from a comfortable distance, but his unwavering gaze soon caught Nana's attention; when Nana approached Ryan to coyly inquire if he was alright, he embarrassingly mumbled that he was fine. When she volunteered that the tour guide in his steady line of sight was a close friend of hers named Tamara, Ryan immediately blushed at the comment. Nana chuckled and, before moving away, told him not to worry, that she would be happy to introduce him to her at the supra. Ryan could not recall when he had felt quite as humiliated as at that moment; nevertheless, a wry smile soon appeared as he anticipated the opportunity to meet this captivating young lady.

Back at the park prior to the beginning of the supra, Ryan spotted Tamara having an animated conversation with another young lady; he immediately looked around to see if he could find Nana, but, not seeing her anywhere, he decided to take fate into his own hands, and approached the two girls. Not speaking much Georgian, he introduced himself in his fluent Russian, which all Georgians in those days spoke, albeit reluctantly; both of the ladies smilingly responded in Russian with their names, but Ryan gave the bulk of his attention to Tamara. Shortly, the other lady politely excused herself, and Ryan and Tamara continued their conversation; eventually, Nana caught sight of Ryan and, grinning widely, concluded that Ryan had become too impatient to wait for her introduction. Not willing to miss the chance to subtly pull his chain, Nana came up to them, gave her friend Tamara a hug, and told her that she was serving as Ryan's interpreter; before moving on, Nana gave Tamara a wink, and assured her in Georgian that Ryan was a good guy.

As the supra was announced and the multitude of guests were invited to the tables, Ryan asked if Tamara would join him, inquiring if perhaps she could help to translate the many toasts that the Tamada would be offering so that he could keep track. She gladly agreed. As with every Georgian supra, the event was pleasantly boisterous, the meal superb, and the toasts were seemingly endless, all accompanied by the mandatory goblet of wine; these, according to local custom, were consumed to the bottom of the goblet, at least in the case of the male participants. Needless to say, by the time the supra finally concluded, none of the participants were feeling any pain, Ryan especially; when Tamara bade him farewell, smiling and offering her hand, Ryan felt a moment of panic, since he had not taken the appropriate opportunity to suggest another meeting. When she turned to leave, he realized that, in the excitement of the evening, he had not obtained her phone number, nor had he determined in which office of the Ministry she worked; he knew that he would need to ask Nana for her help, and that she would playfully embrace the opportunity to make him work as hard as possible for that valuable information.

The next day being Sunday, Madigan spent most of his time reflecting upon the events of the previous day; he had certainly not anticipated that it would be so impactful. Being on the eve of his 32nd birthday and having always been attractive to females, Ryan had certainly experienced romantic intrigue previously, but he had never before felt the stinging impact of "love at first sight." Feeling like a fish out of water, he was actually not quite sure how to handle it. Ever since his near death phenomenon, he was quick to think that his meeting with Tamara might be thanks to the hands of Fate, but he did not want to jump to conclusions, especially since he had no idea if his interest in her was reciprocal. Her response to him had betrayed some level of interest, but her demeanor had been much more controlled than must have been evident in his own puppy-like enthusiasm.

With Nana's help, Ryan was able to track down his newly-found romantic interest; owing to the fact that she was educated as a medical doctor, Tamara's position within the Ministry of Defense was as a staff assistant to the Chief of Medical Policy. Nana provided her phone number and office location that Monday morning, but it took another day or two for Ryan to take action; finally, he garnered up the courage to make a phone call, re-introduce himself, and invite her to dinner later that week. Thankfully, contrary to Madigan's trepidations, she graciously accepted the invitation; the brave combat veteran breathed a deep sigh of relief and had to smile at his own cowardice at the thought of rejection.

The first private dinner date, accompanied by some dancing to a lively Georgian band, was a huge success. Having learned that Georgian women were very traditional, Ryan went out of his way to be the perfect gentleman, and he perceived that his demeanor was well-received. At the end of a lovely evening, Ryan shook her hand, gave her a quick kiss on the back of her extended palm, and bid her a fond farewell. He was pleased that he had not overtly betrayed the inner emotional turmoil that he was experiencing. On the return drive to his hotel, Madigan knew without any doubt that he was hooked like a hungry fish; he wasn't sure where it all would lead, but he felt more completely alive than he had ever felt before. In acknowledgement of the hand of Fate, Ryan felt the emotion of the moment welling up as a few tears rolled down his face; he then whispered a brief but deeply felt "thank you, Dad."

Chapter VII:

When Tamara returned home after her dinner with Madigan, her parents and sister were still awake and chatting in the living room, trying not to appear that they were waiting for her. When she had first told them that she was having dinner that evening with a "nice American military man" whom she had recently met, she did not indicate overtly that it was any big deal. However, there was something in the way she said it that betrayed to her family there might be more here than meets the eye. Over the course of her 25 years, Tamara had indeed had numerous male friends, but she never had even slightly indicated any romantic interest in any of them. Perhaps it was no more than the twinkle in her eye that caught her family's attention, but something was clearly different about this one; their curiosity would not allow them to retire for the evening without more information.

When her mother invited her to join them for a cup of tea, Tamara politely declined and said that she was tired and wanted to go to bed. When her father intervened and tried to persuade her to join them, she declined again. However, her sister was then more abrupt, and simply informed Tamara that she was not going to be allowed to go to bed until she told them about the evening. Always patient and understanding, Tamara smiled shyly and joined the family gathering. She allowed the subtle interrogation to persist for 10-15 minutes, volunteering only that she had met him at the Ministry picnic, had found him to be a pleasant and polite man, and quite handsome as well. She also reported that he was an Afghanistan war veteran who had been wounded and eventually discharged from the Army, but who had volunteered to join the American team helping to advise the Georgian Ministry of Defense. Other than that, Tamara said that she did not know that much about his background, but that she had enjoyed his company. She stated that she did not know if they would see each other socially, simply saying "we shall see." Having finally been freed by her curious family to go to her room, Tamara coyly smiled to herself, curled up with her pillow, and felt an inner contentment as she had never felt before.

Over the following few weeks and months, Ryan and Tamara saw each other sparingly, only as their busy work schedules allowed; both being first time romantics, however, they felt a need to be cautious and not to set their expectations too high. In fact, Madigan found himself away from Tbilisi for training exercises much of the time, and Tamara also had a busy work schedule with many family obligations as well. Nevertheless, they did speak by phone several times per week, and the few social outings that they were able to have continued to underline their mutual feelings that theirs had the potential to be a special relationship.

This being the Fall of 2003, it was also a time of political murmurings and increasing discontent with the status quo in the Republic of Georgia. President Eduard Shevardnadze was becoming increasingly unpopular inside of the country due to generally perceived ineffectiveness as well as charges of serious corruption inside of the government; during October and November of 2003, political opposition became much more widespread and demonstrative. Political fervor came to a head with extremely vocal protests being staged in Tbilisi over the disputed parliamentary elections of November 2nd, in which the opposition party to Shevardnadze was allegedly cheated of victory. This culminated 20 days later with the so-called Rose Revolution in which political opposition led by Mikheil Saakashvili had burst into Parliament with roses in their hands demanding the immediate resignation of President Shevardnadze. With the military forces within the country largely supporting the demonstrators, the writing was on the wall; President Shevardnadze resigned from office on November 22nd, to be succeeded by Saakashvili two months later.

Although the political upheaval made social interaction between Ryan and Tamara more difficult during those two months, it helped to make the excitement of their budding relationship even more intense. Although their official positions made any political activity impossible, both were inherent romantic idealists and enthusiastic followers of the political process, which they hoped would yield national improvements. All Georgians of voting age had already witnessed the rapid evolutionary change from Soviet rule to national independence, the subsequent civil war, and the frustrating political stagnation of the Shevardnadze regime; now they were more than ready to achieve the freedoms and national progress which true democracy promised, and they all hoped and believed that they were now on the cusp of finally achieving their long-awaited goals.

Living in Gomi, outside of the mainstream of the political activity, and dependent upon newscasts that were generally supportive of the Shevardnadze government, Ksenia depended on "inside" news from her family in Tbilisi to stay informed of developments. Her most dependable source in this regard was her favorite granddaughter, Tamara, who drove out to visit her about every two weeks. Having recently turned 80, and having been born just two years after Georgia's previous period of independence was squashed by Soviet Russia's intervention, Ksenia was keenly interested by the Rose Revolution and the dream of true democracy and economic growth that it potentially promised. Tamara's visits afforded her the opportunity to stay current of the dramatic political developments taking place in Tbilisi, as well as to keep track of how her family was surviving in the midst of such chaotic change.

Ksenia had also been informed by her son and daughter-in-law of their as yet unfounded suspicion that Tamara may have met a young man of some special interest. Whereas Tamara had been intentionally vague to her immediate family concerning her true feelings about Ryan Madigan, upon the promise of confidentiality from her trusted soulmate, "Baba" (grandmother) Ksenia, Tamara was more forthcoming with her. She confided to Ksenia that she had never previously been as interested in any other man. She then asked her grandmother many questions about her life with her late husband, Gurgena, about the topic of romantic love in general, and inquired of her opinions of the possible challenges of a relationship with a non-Georgian man. Patient and forthcoming as always, Ksenia admitted that she was not in the position to comment on a relationship with a foreigner, but, knowing Tamara as well as she did, she assured her favorite granddaughter that her heart would guide her properly, and advised her to listen to the innate wisdom of her soul. If this American was the right man with whom to build a life, she would surely know with time. Ksenia added that, at the appropriate time, she hoped that Tamara would introduce her to him.

The first few months of 2004 were exciting ones for Tamara and Ryan. They witnessed the inauguration of Mikheil Saakashvili as President, and they were both enthused by the prospects this held for Georgia. With Ryan's field training requirements being lessened by the onslaught of winter, they saw each other more frequently, and their relationship deepened. It was during February that Ryan first divulged his strong feelings for Tamara, and she for him. Love blossomed during those cold winter months, during which Tamara chose to introduce Ryan to her immediate family; they in turn witnessed the warmth that Tamara clearly felt for this young man, and they were genuinely happy for her. For his part, Madigan got to know her entire family well over several outings and dinners, and he came to witness the deep, loving connection that Tamara's family possessed. Again, he realized the role that Fate had played for him, and he was happy, and at peace, with that knowledge.

In early May of that year, their relationship hit a bump in the road. Ryan learned that his mother had been diagnosed with the early stages of colon cancer, and this created a true dilemma for him. He was torn by his desire to return home to assist his mother during this difficult time, and the obvious reluctance to leave Georgia and his new relationship. It was Tamara who convinced him that he needed to return home to help his mother, with the promise that their love would not suffer by his absence; if their relationship was truly meant to be, the distance between them would not affect them, but rather offer them the opportunity to further analyze whether they were meant to be together. True love would persevere, she had said, and their absence from each other would not impair them. Although they had not yet openly discussed the prospects of marriage, they both knew in their hearts that it was their ultimate destiny, and, if so, this minor interruption would not make any lasting difference.

Ryan explained his situation to his team management, and his company was fully sympathetic; not only would they be able to introduce a replacement to work with the Special Forces Brigade, but they would also place him in an appropriate project administrative position back in their Northern Virginia headquarters, where he could be close to his mother and still contribute to the MOD contract. Under the circumstances, this seemed like the perfect resolution to his dilemma, and his departure was planned for late May. Ryan and Tamara made the most of their time together prior to his departure, with the promise that this absence between them would be brief. On May 27th, Ryan was escorted to Tbilisi International Airport by Tamara and her family; as he returned home, he felt pained by the dual realities, his mother's fight with cancer and the impending absence from Tamara that he was about to face.

Back in the United States, Madigan went directly to his mother's home in Chevy Chase. She was there, having returned just the day before from her initial chemotherapy treatment. She was doing poorly, having had several bouts of nausea that day from the chemo treatment, but she was overjoyed to have Ryan home. Mary Ellen reported that her prognosis was positive; they had caught the cancer early enough, thanks to her recent colonoscopy, and concluded that it should be treatable without any major surgery. Ryan was naturally relieved to receive the positive news, and pleased that he was home to be able to assist his mother through this difficult period. Although he had corresponded with his mother regularly during his stay in Georgia, his communications with her had been admittedly lacking in full detail, other than he was enjoying his work assignment and life in general. Now that he had time to fill in the many blanks, he was able to tell her about his relationship with Tamara and to patiently and fully answer the myriad of questions that resulted from his revelation.

Mary Ellen was cautious in her enthusiasm until he had answered most of her questions. As far as she knew, this was Ryan's first serious romantic relationship; although he had always been popular with females, she had secretly even begun to wonder what was his real sexual preference, so she was pleased to hear of this news. God willing, she might finally have some grandchildren! Ryan described the activities of the last few months in great detail, from his work with the Special Forces Brigade, to his impressions of Georgia in general, and, of course, his fateful meeting with Tamara and getting to know her and her family. He confided that he had never felt this way about any other girl before, and, although he stopped short of confirming his desire to marry her, he revealed that he had never been happier in his life. He did tell her that he hoped to have Tamara come to the States for a visit this coming summer, and that he was anxious to introduce her to his mother, family and friends.

The next few months passed slowly. He missed Tamara a great deal, and he corresponded with her daily either by phone or email. Mary Ellen continued with her chemotherapy treatment on a regular basis, and her doctors informed her and Ryan that the prognosis continued to look positive; they believed that they had caught the disease in time, and that it was in remission from her treatment. Ryan's new job in the office environment was not as interesting as working in the field, but he was appreciative that the company had been able to accommodate his transfer so generously. Happily, his successor in Tbilisi was apparently doing well with the SF Brigade, and the project was moving ahead successfully. He and Tamara had agreed that she should visit him in the States in August; she would be able to take leave from the Ministry and Ryan could also take time off, so she had applied for her visitor's visa, about which she expected to hear soon. All in all, life was going as well as could be planned.

When the time came for Tamara to arrive in early August, Madigan's apprehension was electric. He was so excited by the prospect of seeing her again that he didn't sleep for days before her arrival; he was also a bit apprehensive that his mother might not take to her as well as he hoped, but he understood that there was not much he could do about that possibility. Everyone seemed to love Tamara, so he was confident that Mary Ellen would fall into line quickly too.

He met Tamara at Dulles International Airport alone, and he had arranged, with his mother's blessing, that they would spend their first few days alone on a short trip; he wanted to show her some of the beautiful Virginia surroundings, as well as to get reacquainted. From the airport, after her late afternoon arrival, Ryan took Tamara on a drive to the charming nearby village of Middleburg, where they would stay in an historic country inn with a renowned restaurant on the premises. Although she was tired from the trip, their conversation throughout the evening was excited and animated; after a romantic dinner, they retired to their beautiful room, furnished with 18th century antiques, where they talked and snuggled late into the night, until peaceful fatigue finally overcame both of them.

The next morning, after a late breakfast, Ryan took her on a drive south on the Blue Ridge Parkway, a scenic trip interrupted by frequent stops to enjoy the beautiful views of the Shenandoah Valley; he had reserved a room at another Bed and Breakfast Inn close to Wintergreen resort, and dined at a nearby brew pub that Ryan had enjoyed the last time he had visited the nearby Monroe Institute. The day had been perfect in terms of weather, with sunny blue skies and a cooler than usual temperature for an August day, followed by another magical evening in which love and excitement make time pass too quickly, yet create perfection when the day ends in each other's arms. Ryan's last waking thought before falling into a deep and blissful sleep was that he had truly found the person with whom he wanted to spend every day for the remainder of his life.

Although he had been tempted several times over the past 6 months to reveal to Tamara the story of his near death experience, he had ultimately decided that the time to do so had not yet arrived; he had told her of the severity of his injuries in Afghanistan, and that he was in a coma for an extended period of time, but he had ultimately decided to save the harder-to-believe aspects for another time. Since Ryan had decided that he wanted to take her to the Monroe Institute to visit the next day, he chose to tell her the entire story that following morning. He took her to nearby Crabtree Falls, having decided it would be an appropriate spot to have such a conversation; the falls created such a majestic spirit-expanding atmosphere that Madigan believed it would be the perfect spot in which to reveal his credibility-challenged story. Ryan had pre-selected a place near the cascades of the falls which he believed would create the proper atmosphere for his revelation, private, yet not too loud to drown out the fine points of his story. In keeping with the old Army adage, "prior planning prevents piss-poor performance," he had chosen well.

Madigan had also planned his revelation carefully, to gradually introduce those elements of his saga that might cause the highest probability of disbelief, and to pause to allow for questions at each transition point. Surprisingly, Tamara listened attentively, nodding empathetically without posing any questions through the duration of his expose; even the out-of-body conversation with his late father did not seem to evoke any untoward expressions of disbelief from Tamara. When he had finally finished his story, he sat silently for another minute to allow Tamara the opportunity to raise questions; when none came, he finally, carefully, asked her if she believed him. Tamara simply smiled in response, said that of course she believed him, and then told him that he was not the first person to tell her of similar near death experiences; she continued to say that two of her patients during her medical residency had had similar experiences, and that she was convinced of their veracity. Madigan drew an intense sigh of relief, and then sat back to listen to her further explanation.

By the time she had completed her two stories, and conveyed her full impressions to Ryan, it was getting close to sunset; there was not time to pay their visit to the Monroe Institute, so they postponed it until the next day. After a quiet dinner at another local restaurant, during which animated conversation mostly gave way to quiet reflection, they returned to their bed and breakfast inn, and got into bed relatively early; they spoke softly through much of the night until sleep finally overcame them. Both fell asleep in their lover's arms convinced that life had indeed purposely brought them together, just as it was certainly intended to be.

When they visited Monroe Institute the next morning, Tamara was fascinated by the peaceful, yet energy-driven atmosphere, the far-reaching library of books and audio versions on spiritual topics, as well as the wide curriculum of intriguing courses that they offered. Tamara stated that she could definitely spend much of her life there, as long as Ryan was with her, of course. Ryan also introduced her to the instructors and advisors that he had previously met there, and the day, full of captivating conversation, passed all too quickly. They spent their final night at the bed and breakfast, this time sleeping soundly and completely after an eventful and exhausting couple of days, and drove back to Chevy Chase the next morning to meet Mary Ellen. During that several hour drive, Madigan matter-of-factly told Tamara that he wanted to marry her; she looked at him intently for what seemed like endless seconds, before replying, "I thought you'd never ask."

Chapter VIII:

Ryan and Tamara had arrived at Mary Ellen's home in Chevy Chase several days previously. Ryan had been rife with trepidation that his mother might not, for one or another reason, be so enamored with Tamara; he had also started to second guess the timing of his proposal of marriage, thinking that it might have been wiser to wait until Tamara and Mary Ellen had the opportunity to meet. As it turned out, he had worried in vain; Mary Ellen and Tamara hit it off from the very first moment, and had happily chattered away for hours on end, nearly to the complete exclusion of Ryan. He even felt a slight twinge of jealousy at how well they were getting along, without seeming to need his participation; realizing his misjudgment, however, he glanced skyward and silently thanked his dad again for looking out for him.

On the fourth day home, Ryan decided, after consultation with Tamara, that it was time to inform his mother about their plans to be married. Upon hearing the news, Mary Ellen was beside herself with joy and excitement, screaming like a young girl on her first roller coaster ride; after the exultation died down, she hugged them both desperately and, with tears streaming down her cheeks, wryly asked Ryan, "what took you so long?"

Tamara was due to return to Tbilisi a few days later; the final days of her visit were split between sight-seeing in Washington, DC, and discussing wedding plans and the difficult logistics with family members and friends spread halfway around the world. Concerning visa considerations for Tamara, although this would entail some lengthy periods of separation, they ultimately decided that they would hold the wedding in Washington. Since Ryan knew the American Ambassador to Georgia as well as several of the Consular Officers in the Embassy in Tbilisi, he believed that he should be able to expedite the normally lengthy fiance visa process so that she would be able to join him in the USA no later than the following spring. In the meantime, he hoped that he would be able to finagle a business trip or two to Georgia for project follow-up; time would tell.

When Tamara returned to Tbilisi, Ryan felt like his world had been stripped away from him; he experienced loneliness like he had never felt before, and the daily phone calls and emails only alleviated the pain for brief periods of time. He had his mother to help to assuage his feelings of emptiness, and his work kept his mind somewhat occupied on other topics, but the days were long, and his nights were lacking in the complete companionship he had felt with Tamara close to him. Time in general passed slowly, but he kept his dreams alive in the planning for his future when he and Tamara would be reunited. In this respect, Mary Ellen was the strong foundation in his life; her enthusiastic assistance with the planning process was both invaluable and highly appreciated. In fact, he began to feel as if he had never been closer to his mother, and their relationship flourished.

Ryan was able to reserve a date at the Georgetown University Chapel for the wedding, which he tentatively set for April, 2005. Knowing that, even with his influence in the American Embassy in Tbilisi, the K-1 fiance visa process would be bureaucratically lengthy, he had timed Tamara's arrival with the worst case scenario in mind. The visa was estimated to require about 6 months; with the wedding required by law to take place within 90 days of Tamara's arrival in the USA, he felt safe that his April wedding date would be timed well. He also managed to arrange a business trip to Tbilisi for October, so their absence from each other would happily be relatively brief.

His trip to Georgia could not come fast enough for Ryan. The lengthy voyage from Washington to Tbilisi, via Frankfurt, seemed to take an eternity; having departed Dulles International Airport on Friday evening, with an 8-hour layover in Frankfurt, he did not arrive in Tbilisi until 0330 on Sunday morning. Tamara was there waiting for him, and the sight of her, for the first time in over two months, immediately cured the fatigue from the trip and the emptiness he had felt for so long. She drove him to his old hotel, the Sheraton Metechi Palace, where they went immediately to his room; they spent the next few hours in animated conversation, before finally falling into a deep and restful sleep later that morning. Tamara's family had a supra planned for him that evening, so they were able to spend most of the entire day locked blissfully in each other's arms.

Tamara's family touted the Sunday evening supra as an engagement celebration. They held the dinner at a traditional Georgian restaurant on the banks of the Mtkvari River, which flows through the center of Tbilisi, and nearly the entire family was in attendance; the only exception was Tamara's beloved grandmother, Ksenia, who had fallen ill and could not attend. Naturally, Tamara's father assumed the position of Tamada, and the marvelous Georgian feast was augmented by a lengthy litany of eloquent toasts in the best Georgian fashion. Although still fatigued from the lengthy trip, Ryan was ebullient with the festivities and the gregarious warmth and acceptance he was given by his extended family-to-be. The supra went late into the night before Ryan, happily inebriated with the love of family and more than an adequate consumption of Georgian wine, finally was driven back to his hotel for a few hours of sleep before reporting to the Ministry of Defense the next morning.

Madigan's work schedule was busy the entire week conducting project reviews with his company's contractor team, as well as meetings with various officers of the Ministry of Defense; when he was free for lunch, he was always able to meet with Tamara to catch up, and to bring her with him to the several dinners they had with Ministry officials. At the conclusion of the hectic week, Ryan and Tamara were able to sneak off to a resort hotel in Kazbegi, situated in a picturesque mountainous region of Georgia, where they spent nearly two days before returning to Tbilisi on Sunday morning to catch his 0500 flight to Munich with connections back to Dulles Airport. His two flights required crossing 8 time zones and 16 hours in duration, so, when he finally disembarked in Washington, he was indeed exhausted, but ecstatically happy with the time he had spent with Tamara and her family.

It would be another 4 long months before Ryan would be able to see his fiancé again; although he had maintained hopes of speeding up the process, the issuance of the K-1 visa was subject to an unsympathetic bureaucracy which was clearly resistant to change. Hundreds of phone calls and emails helped to abate the pain of the lengthy absence; the day would finally come in early March, 2005, that Tamara disembarked at Dulles to begin the next chapter with the love of her life.

The wedding was set for April 15th, 2005, at Georgetown's charming Dahlgren Chapel, right in the heart of the University campus. The intimate chapel was the perfect setting for the wedding ceremony, which was attended by a small gathering of family and friends; Ryan had a couple of buddies from school days, and a few family members, while Tamara's sister and uncle were able to travel from Georgia to attend. Following the Catholic ceremony, all gathered at the nearby 1789 Restaurant for a private dinner; whereas the number of menu items and wine consumption were lesser in comparison to Georgian standards, the love enveloping the private room was no less in intensity. Once the evening had ended, Ryan and Tamara retired to their recently rented home in Northern Virginia, and left the next morning to spend a few days in Hot Springs, Virginia, at the famously luxurious Homestead Hotel.

After a wonderful honeymoon at The Homestead, Ryan and Tamara returned to the Washington area to begin their lives together as Mr. and Mrs. Ryan O'Roarke Madigan. While Ryan remained positively employed with the same defense contracting business, Tamara, who had graduated from medical school and completed her residency in Tbilisi before working as a health advisor with the Ministry of Defense, began the lengthy process to become accredited as a practicing physician in the United States. This process entailed a number of challenging tests which required months of study not only to be able to translate her Georgian medical education into American standards and practices, but also to do so in a foreign language, in which she was not yet comfortably fluent. Once she completed her studies sufficient to be able to pass the numerous and complicated tests, a process which could require at least one year, then she would need to complete her residency once again, this time in the USA, in order to be licensed to practice medicine. In all, Tamara faced a two to three-year process to earn her medical certification, but this did not faze her in the least; although she did miss her family in Georgia, overall she had never felt such happiness. Her life with Ryan was everything she had ever dared to hope for.

The next three years were largely standard issue, happy yet normal daily routines, interspersed with a few special occasions to introduce diversity into one's life. At the outset, Tamara was very busy studying and preparing for the medical certification tests, and, once she passed the tests, hard at work for long hours fulfilling her USA residency requirements. The all-too-infrequent free time together with Ryan provided her the joy and energy to maintain the tedious pace to complete her medical certification. Ryan had an equally busy schedule in his job, which did not seem quite as purposeful as the path that Tamara was following, but he did honestly enjoy the work (at least most of the time) and it was providing the financial means to support Tamara's training and normal household requirements. To suggest that Ryan's and Tamara's life was all work and no play would not be a fair assessment; as much as possible, they tried to devote evenings and the week-ends to themselves, although they visited with Mary Ellen at least one or two times per week. The most telling tale of their life over these years was that neither of them ever complained, and both were simply highly content with life, and the love that they shared.

During these three years, travel back to Georgia for either

Tamara or Ryan became nearly impossible. Tamara's medical studies kept her quite occupied so that the communications with her family were limited to emails, phone calls and Skype. Ryan's foreign travel was also curtailed quite a bit; he did make a couple of trips as part of the company team to investigate new defense projects in other countries, but he made only one trip back to Georgia during this time period; that was in August of 2006. Although he was largely pre-occupied with work requirements during this trip, he was able to break away to spend time with Tamara's family on a couple of occasions; this included a family supra at the dacha of Tamara's uncle, David, where Ryan finally met Tamara's favorite grandmother, Ksenia. Tamara had pleaded with Ryan to please give Baba Ksenia a big hug for her, and to assure her that her granddaughter was happy and thriving in America, but that she loved and missed her Baba terribly. The happiness in Ksenia's demeanor at all of his reassuring news, plus the numerous tears of joy that escaped her wise, vibrant eyes, made Ryan fully comprehend how uniquely close was the relationship between Tamara and Ksenia, and it thoroughly warmed his heart.

In addition to the warming of the weather and the blossoming of nature that indicates the emergence of spring, May 2008 brought several significant events into the lives of Mr. and Mrs. Ryan Madigan. Firstly, Tamara completed her medical residency and she was finally to be fully certified as a practicing physician in the USA. Earlier that year, she had also taken the pledge of allegiance to become a citizen of the United States, so she felt that she had crossed several important bridges by the time May came around. Tamara's younger brother, Irakli, had also recently gotten engaged to be married, with the wedding having been set for early

September, 2008, in Tbilisi. Tamara was incredibly excited that she and Ryan would be able to travel there together; it had been three years since she had seen her family, and she couldn't wait to see everyone again.

Other than work, visiting his mother as often as he could, and simply enjoying married life, Ryan devoted as much time as possible to staying in touch with his spiritual self. He meditated daily, usually soon after awakening while Tamara still slept, he continued to research near death and out-of-body phenomena, and he maintained contact with the instructors at the Monroe Institute whom he had befriended previously. Over this time period, he found that he would still, on rare occasion, awake with the realization that he had dreamed about an out-of-body episode during the night, each time with puzzling aspects that he struggled to place into proper perspective. During a rare extended weekend, he and Tamara had also paid a visit to Monroe Institute to recharge themselves from the ambiance of deep spirituality there and to visit with valued friends.

Back in Georgia, the spring and summer of 2008 paid witness to troubling times, especially as they pertained to the country's relationship with Russia. Political rhetoric between the two countries was becoming dangerously high-pitched, and there were murmurings that Russian President Medvedev, influenced by Prime Minister Putin, wanted to instigate regime change in Georgia to eliminate President Saakhashvili. How far the Russians might move in this direction was the question in everyone's mind who had a stake in this small, relatively insignificant nation on the eastern coast of the Black Sea.

Chapter IX:

During the time following the 2003 Rose Revolution and the election of Mikheil Saakashvili as President in early 2004, relations between Russia and Georgia deteriorated significantly. Paramount in this development was Saakashvili's aggressive moves towards his desired alliance with western nations, and, most significantly, his desire for Georgia to become a member of NATO. Russia was particularly disturbed with increased efforts by the United States Government to support Georgia's efforts in this regard, as evidenced by the USA GTEP program to enhance Georgia's military capabilities, and by their active endorsement of Georgia's application for NATO. Russian President Medvedev and Prime Minister Putin had openly declared that neighboring Georgia would never be allowed to join NATO, but had not yet initiated any visible efforts to prevent the Georgian leadership from proceeding to do so.

Playing a major role in this political dilemma was the concurrent desire of the regions of South Ossetia and Abkhazia to gain their official independence from Georgia. President Saakashvili had made the full and final integration of these semi-autonomous regions into Georgia as one of the mandates of his Presidential administration. Simultaneously, Russia had been meddling in these regions for years and using them as political pawns in its ongoing dispute with Georgia. In March of 2008, both South Ossetia and Abkhazia submitted formal requests to Russia to recognize their aspirations of independence from Georgia; in response to their requests, later that month, the Russian Duma adopted a resolution to consider official Russian recognition of independence for these two regions. In April, Russian leadership indicated that it would support these requests and would expand their official ties with both regions, moves which infuriated the Georgian President.

Over the next several months, international political activity revolving around these two regions intensified, as Russia moved to recognize their independence and increase its political influence and military involvement, particularly in South Ossetia. In early July, military skirmishes began to break out between South Ossetian and Georgian forces, and all sides began to respond with increasingly defiant political rhetoric and preparations for the possibility of full military conflict. For its part, the Georgian Ministry of Defense made plans to increase the size of its military, including the call-up of active reserve forces to counter the threat of Russian aggression. As a result, thousands of Georgian reservists were called to active duty during July. This included Tamara Madigan's younger brother, Irakli, who had been trained as a reserve Army communications specialist; although his wedding date was set for only 6 weeks hence, Irakli entered active duty with the Georgian Army in mid-July, 2008.

It was only a matter of time before the intense political rhetoric between Russia, Georgia and South Ossetia, aided and abetted by increased involvement of the divided international community, would evolve into full-scale military confrontation. Throughout July, Russia had begun staging military forces along its southern border with Georgia/South Ossetia, and gave every indication to the Georgian leadership that it was fully prepared to support South Ossetia in its quest for independence. President

Saakashvili had issued a call for help to the United States and its western allies, but the collective western wisdom was for Georgia to allow diplomacy to take its full course. However, when South Ossetian forces began the shelling of ethnic Georgian villages on the evening of August 7th, Saakashvili was forced to authorize a full-scale military operation to counter their aggression, a move that ultimately let loose the dogs of war.

Georgian forces entered South Ossetian territory during the early morning hours of August 8th. Their mission was three-fold, to counter and negate the shelling of ethnic Georgian villages within South Ossetia, to offer protection to those same ethnic Georgians, and to prevent the entry of positioned Russian forces into South Ossetia from the north. Whereas Georgia had sent sufficient forces into South Ossetia to possibly handle two of the three missions they had been assigned, they were entirely undermanned and ill-equipped to face a possible incursion of many thousands of Russian troops; since the Russians would need to enter Ossetia via tunnels and bridges that formed strategic bottlenecks for the movement of their forces, Georgia's chances for a positive result depended upon controlling those strategic points, and closing them off to Russian advance.

The focal point of the Georgian incursion was the South Ossetian capital city of Tskhinvali; it was situated in a natural valley surrounded by highlands that enveloped numerous traditionally ethnic Georgian villages. It was also the city into which the main strategic tributary, the Roki Tunnel, would potentially empty thousands of well-equipped and well-trained Russian forces into the heart of the struggle for control of South Ossetia. At the same time that Georgian forces began to cross the border with Ossetia to move towards Tskhinvali and its surrounding highlands, Russian forces were mobilizing to move across their border with South Ossetia to join the fight. The Georgian forces that had been deployed to move into South Ossetia were about 10,000 in numbers, divided among several brigades and numerous smaller operational units; the Russian forces threatening to make their way south to confront them were two to three times larger, and multiple times more lethal in capability. The fate of the two opposing forces would rest largely on who would reach Roki Tunnel first with large enough numbers to control ingress and egress from it.

While the Georgian conventional forces and their supporting armor and artillery units were methodically making their way northward towards Tskhinvali, several operational detachments of the Georgian Special Forces Brigade had infiltrated Ossetian territory in advance. Their assignments were for reconnaissance and strategic special intervention purposes revolving around Roki Tunnel, which provided the sole route for adequate vehicular access from the Russian region of Northern Ossetia into South Ossetia through the Caucasus Mountains. One operational SF detachment was deployed into Ossetia during the early morning hours of August 8th, with the mission to emplace and explode demolitions within the southern portion of Roki Tunnel before Russian forces could use it to reach Tskhinvali. Another smaller detachment was infiltrated to the area overlooking the northern entrance of Roki Tunnel, which was located in Russian territory, for reconnaissance purposes; their mission was to identify Russian units enroute to South Ossetia and to report their tactical strength to MOD HQs. On this smaller detachment were three Special Forces soldiers and one attached communications specialist whose sole purpose was to set up the commo equipment and report team reconnaissance findings to Tbilisi; the communications specialist assigned to the SF detachment was Irakli Donauri, Ryan Madigan's brother-in-law.

The two SF detachments were infiltrated under cover of darkness into Ossetian territory via UH-1H helicopters; they flew north from Tbilisi generally following the route of the Georgian Military Highway as far as Gudauri until veering west into South Ossetia. The two teams were inserted at different pre-planned locations. The Roki Tunnel demolition detachment was landed and deployed not far from the south tunnel entrance, to where they continued on foot through forested terrain. The reconnaissance mini-detachment was flown into the mountainous territory on the north slope of the Caucasus, where the team repelled from their helicopter onto the rocky terrain below; from there, they hiked several kilometers to a pre-selected position providing a line-of-sight view of the northern entrance of the tunnel.

Just as the sun was beginning to rise on the early morning of August 8th, the recon team settled into their observation post position that provided adequate cover and concealment of their presence either from land or possible Russian aircraft. As the SF soldiers were settling into their observation positions, Irakli set up his communications equipment to enable timely reporting of the vital tactical intelligence that they hoped to convey to Georgian military and civilian leadership.

Even though he was a reservist, Irakli was very well suited for his role as a communications specialist on this important mission; his civilian job was as an IT expert, working for the

Georgian equivalent of the USA National Security Agency, specializing in satellite communications. The equipment that he was carrying for this mission included a handheld Harris radio with encryption software, a 20-watt pocket amplifier to boost his transmissions, a portable SATCOM antenna, and several portable batteries, enough to enable many hours of operation. Once established in his position, and having set up his equipment to maximize satellite reception, he performed a test burst and confirmed that he was fully operational.

As the sun began to rise on that morning of August 8th, 2008, both SF detachments were in position and ready to carry out their separate missions to the best of their ability; and, as the sun rose on the northern slope of the Caucasus Mountains, many thousands of truck-mounted Russian soldiers, intermixed with dozens of tanks and mobile artillery pieces, began to move south through the 3.6-mile-long Roki Tunnel into South Ossetia.

By the time that they had arrived on site, just before sunrise, the Georgian SF Detachment deployed to set and detonate explosives in the southern end of the Roki Tunnel could already hear the oncoming traffic steadily approaching thru the tunnel. Just after the Georgians had managed to emplace a handful of electronic explosive devices, the Russians had come upon them, spotted them and opened fire. The lead vehicles were machine gun mounted armored personnel carriers, with Russian Spetsnaz troops therein, intended to confront and clear any initial opposition that they might face. The Georgian team members returned fire, but the odds were against them and they were forced to flee for safety; they were not able to detonate the explosives without killing themselves, so they fled with the hope that they might find another opportunity. Two of the detachment members were hit badly, and did not make it out of the tunnel; the remainder were able to reach the forested slope outside the tunnel before the Russians emerged.

Meanwhile, the recon team surveilling the north end of the tunnel witnessed an unrelenting parade of Russian APCs, tanks and artillery pieces entering the tunnel; Irakli had managed to transmit situation reports every 15-20 minutes in their effort to keep the Georgian MOD leadership advised on a timely basis. Russian aircraft periodically flew overhead into Ossetian territory, forcing the recon team below to hunker down and maintain their concealment, somewhat impeding their ability to transmit their sitreps. After they had been in place for a little more than two hours, a Russian Mi-24 helicopter gunship flew nearby, a few hundred meters east of their location and just above treetop level; the team froze motionless in position until the helicopter had passed a kilometer to the south. A few minutes later, to their dismay, the soldiers noticed that the chopper had suddenly turned and was heading back in their direction, on a course to pass directly overhead.

The SF detachment at the south end of the tunnel took cover on the forested slope about 50 meters from the tunnel exit and assumed firing positions; the engineers in the team attempted to detonate the few explosives they had managed to emplace using their cell phone detonation devices, but they had lost sufficient unobstructed line-of-sight to be able to do so. Once the Russian vehicles began to emerge from the tunnel, the Georgians opened fire. The first three APCs to emerge from the tunnel veered off of the main road towards the Georgian positions, assumed attack positions, and returned heavy machine gun fire. The Georgians, outnumbered and outgunned, returned steady fire, but soon realized the futility of their situation, and began to retreat farther up the slope into the deeper forest. The Russian Spetsnaz soldiers inside of the APCs began to disembark from their protective vehicles and to deploy into tactical pursuit of the retreating Georgian detachment. Meanwhile, the parade of Russian military vehicles began to emerge in earnest from the Roki Tunnel, and to continue on their mission towards the capital of Tskhinvali.

The SF Recon detachment observing the north end of the tunnel was hunkered down motionless as the Russian helicopter made its way directly towards their concealed positions. Although they did not believe that they had been spotted, the fact that the armed helicopter gunship was heading directly towards them created a serious "pucker factor." The chopper passed directly overhead, and, about 200 meters past their position, banked again to head back into their direction; now, they began to suspect that the Russian pilots must have detected something of interest. Irakli immediately felt fear as he had never experienced before; he began to think immediately of his family and of his beautiful fiancé who was anxiously awaiting his safe return.

Captain Yuri Popov was in command of the company of Russian Special Forces soldiers who had been assigned to the invasion force; they were officially a sub-unit of the 45th Guards Detached Spetsnaz Brigade, one of Russia's most elite and largely-utilized military units. Captain Popov's was the lead Russian unit making its way through the Roki Tunnel when the opposition forces attempting to obstruct their passage had first been confronted. With the Georgian opposition forces having made their retreat into the heavily-forested hills surrounding the tunnel exit, Captain Popov was directing his Spetsnaz forces in pursuit of the Georgians, as well as calling in air support to assist in the operation. Upon his request, two Mi-24 helicopters, loaded with 2 squads of Spetsnaz forces kept in reserve, took off from Russian territory near the north end of the tunnel to support the fight.

Irakli's recon unit was still frozen in place; the Mi-24 helicopter that had been hovering near their position was still very much in the area, and the Georgians were beginning to come to the realization that the chopper pilot might have detected their presence. In addition, off to the north of their position and heading in their general direction, Irakli detected two more Russian Mi-24 gunships on the horizon. The SF detachment commander had also taken notice and signaled to his teammates that they may need to depart from their position. However, to do so with the Mi-24 so close by would certainly reveal their presence; the detachment commander signaled to hold tight and await an opportunity to move out.

As the two approaching Russian helicopters came within close range of the north tunnel detachment's recon position, with the other Mi-24 still hovering around their position, Irakli noticed that one of the two approaching helicopters began to hover just east of their position, and appeared to be descending, while the other Mi-24 passed by and appeared to be heading south by itself. The descending aircraft was now out of sight, but he could hear that it was still hovering just about 100-200 meters east of their position. Little did he know that rope lines had been lowered and that a team of

Russian Spetsnaz soldiers was now repelling into a cleared area nearby. After a few moments, the rappelling lines had been retrieved and the unloaded Mi-24 became visible again to Irakli, and appeared to be heading south in the same direction as the previous helicopter. At that moment, the gunship that had been hovering over their position fired one of its mounted rockets into the tree line within 20 meters from where two recon spotters had been concealed; shocked by the rocket fire, Irakli still had the presence of mind to transmit a short message to HQs briefly detailing that the team had been spotted and had been fired upon. It was time to begin a hasty retreat from the vicinity.

The recon detachment commander gave the signal to move out. Like the rest of his teammates, Irakli only had time to secure essential gear; this included his radio equipment, but he was not able to devote the time to retrieve his portable antenna. He knew that further commo with HQs would be nearly impossible without it. As they retreated eastward through the tree line, the team tried to make full use of the overhead concealment that the forest offered them. Nevertheless, it was clear that the hovering helicopter had seen their movement, and was following their retreat. Unknown to them was the fact that the chopper pilot was calling out their movements to the Spetsnaz team commander that had rappelled to the ground, and was at that movement moving directly towards them. The trailing chopper was herding them directly towards the approaching Spetsnaz team.

At the southern end of the tunnel, the Georgian Special Forces team that had begun their retreat into the forested hills had, by this time, noticed the arrival of a Russian Mi-24 off to their east. They were still receiving steady fire from the

Russian Spetsnaz soldiers pursuing them from the tunnel, and they had already suffered several fatalities in their team. The men who had assumed the point position in their retreat had line-of-sight view of the Russian helicopter about 200 meters to the east, and were shocked to see that a team of Russian soldiers was rappelling from the chopper to the ground; the realization came to them quickly that their escape route would be blocked, and that they were about to be surrounded by the enemy. The point men rushed to their team commander to advise him of the situation, and the decision was made for the Georgians to assume a defensive position and to try to defend themselves from the Russians approaching from two sides.

Meanwhile, Irakli's recon team was in flight moving east away from their previous position; Irakli noted that the Russian helicopter was still trailing them, and was surprised that the gunship had not fired upon them a second time. It was then that he understood the cat and mouse game in which they were engaged. The Russian helicopter that had descended below his vantage point previously had probably unloaded foot soldiers, and the realization hit him that they were running directly into a potential ambush. Within moments, his thinking became reality as the forest directly in front of them became alive with automatic weapons fire; two of his teammates were hit, and Irakli and his running mate took cover as best they could. He wanted to run to assist his teammates who had been shot, but the steady automatic weapons fire aimed at them prevented any movement. With the Mi-24 gunship hovering overhead, and an obvious superior force blocking their retreat, the sad conclusion became imminently clear. They could fight and die, or surrender their position with the hope of surviving to fight another day. With his two comrades badly hit, and in need of assistance, and just one other teammate available to continue to fight, Irakli took the initiative and yelled his plea in Russian to surrender their arms and forego the fight.

The Georgians at the southern end of the tunnel found themselves quickly in a similar predicament. Russian Spetsnaz forces coming from two directions had managed to surround the defensive position that they had assumed and had begun to inflict heavy fire and casualties on the Georgians. Several team members had already been hit, and the numbers and fire superiority of the Russian forces was making their chances of escape highly unlikely. When the firefight ceased momentarily, and the leader of the Spetsnaz forces presented the opportunity for the Georgians to surrender the fight, the Georgian detachment commander decided that their fate was sealed; he ordered his surviving comrades to throw down their arms, and live to fight another day. Having surrendered to the Russian forces, the detachment commander realized that his team had paid a heavy price; 5 had been killed, another 3 were seriously wounded, and only 4 had escaped serious harm. The Russians called in one of the Mi-24 gunships to land in the nearest clearing to their location, and moved the Georgian prisoners, including those wounded, to the not-too-distant landing zone. They were soon flown to a makeshift prisoner of war and medical facility in the northern portion of Tskinvali, where they were incarcerated.

Irakli's team in the north endured a similar fate. The helicopter that had been dogging them over the past hour found a suitable landing zone close by to the surrender site, and the Russians took their prisoners, both healthy and wounded, to the LZ; from there, they were flown to the same makeshift POW facility in northern Tskinvali. Upon arrival, the wounded Georgians were taken to a nearby medical facility for treatment, and Irakli and his healthy comrade were taken to their cell. The building to which they had been taken was clearly some sort of a police station and jail, but smallish in size, and cell space was limited; in fact, although no words were exchanged, Irakli had noticed a few of his Georgian Special Forces comrades present in the cells. He suffered the sudden realization that their missions to surveill and obstruct the Russian forces entering South Ossetia had failed miserably. Sitting in his cell, Irakli began to ponder what would be their ultimate fate, and whether or not he would ever again see his lovely finance or family.

One of the police officers on duty in the Tskhinvali police station was an officer by the name of Nika Gagloyev, son of an Ossetian father and a Georgian mother. Although he had lived in Tskhinvali much of his life, he had spent 10 of his younger years in primary school and the university in Tbilisi, where his uncle on his mother's side lived. In fact, his cousin, the son of his uncle, had been Nika's constant companion during the time he had lived in Tbilisi, and they had maintained close personal contact despite recent troubles. Nika had noticed that the Georgian soldiers who had been incarcerated wore the Special Forces insignia on their uniform, the same insignia that his cousin, Mamuka, wore on his.

Later that evening, Georgian Special Forces Captain, Vasili Tsintsadze, received a phone call from his cousin, Nika Gagloyev. Nika was very careful and brief in his message to Vasili, lest the phone call might be intercepted. After the 30-second, mostly one-way conversation, Captain Tsintsadze had received the unhappy, yet welcome, news; numerous Georgian Special Forces soldiers had been captured by the Russians and were being held at Nika's "work facility." Captain Tsintsadze immediately rang the SF Brigade Commander, Colonel Roin Dolidze, to advise him of the news that he had just received. In turn, Dolidze contacted his top staff officers to join him in his office in order to brief them on this new intel, and discuss how best to proceed. Roin brought everyone present entirely up to date on what they knew of the situation on the battlefield; he also shared with them the content of the last situation report that the MOD had received from the SF recon detachment who had been watching the Russian advance into the Roki Tunnel. He knew that the recon unit had been spotted and fired upon, but that was the last transmission that had been received. He was also unaware of any reports from the other SF detachment that had been deployed to attempt to obstruct the south end of the tunnel. All he knew was that this first day of conflict with the Russians had not gone entirely well.

Towards day's end, although it was near midnight in Tbilisi, Roin decided to make one more call before he tried to grab a few hours sleep. Knowing that the communications specialist attached to the SF recon detachment, undoubtedly the person who had sent in that last sitrep, was related by marriage to his old friend and American colleague, Ryan Madigan, Roin decided to give Ryan a quick call and bring him as up to date as possible. Ryan received the grave information, thanked his friend for the heads-up, and then sat in reflection for some time trying to decide how best to use this information. When the possible solution finally came to him, a quick look at the watch confirmed that it was only 4:30 in the afternoon on the USA east coast, so he made a call to his friends at the Monroe Institute.

After a quick explanation that he had an emergency that would benefit greatly from their help, an agreement was reached that Ryan would arrive the next morning. He then waited for Tamara to return home from work, so that he could share the unhappy news with her, and explain the action that he planned to take.

Chapter X:

When it had become clear that armed conflict was unavoidable, on August 7th, the Georgian government stationed as many as 16,000 combined Georgian forces on the South Ossetia border; in the early morning hours of August 8th, Georgian forces began their movement into South Ossetia with the planned goal of taking the capital city of Tskhinvali. At that point in time, Tskhinvali was defended by only an estimated 500 South Ossetia soldiers, about 500 Russian soldiers, plus another 250 Russian Peacekeepers, part of the OSCE-designated monitoring force in Ossetia. Although Russian forces began their movement from North to South Ossetia in the early morning of August 8th, the bottleneck created by the Roki Tunnel made the movement of their troops and heavy military equipment a very slow process. As a result, the Georgians enjoyed initial successes in their efforts to take control of Tskhinvali; by early afternoon of August 8th, Georgian forces had captured significant portions of Tskhinvali with the exception of some important parts of the center as well as the northern parts of the city. With the steadily increasing arrival of Russian combat and support units during the day, the tide gradually turned in the favor of the Russians, and the Georgians were gradually forced to withdraw to the southern portions of the city. Fighting had reportedly been vicious on that first full day of fighting, although military fatalities from the fighting were relatively small with both sides each reporting 20-30 soldiers killed in action.

Heavy fighting in and around Tskhinvali continued

throughout August 9th, and into August 10th as well. The Georgians largely managed to maintain their positions in the capital city throughout the 9th and the early part of the 10th, until the steady flow of Russian ground forces, tanks and artillery, and increased sorties of Russian aircraft, finally became too much for the Georgian forces to handle. The tide of the battle for Tskhinvali and control over South Ossetia was too strongly in favor of the Russians, and, by the evening of August 10th, Georgian President Saakashvili declared a cease fire on behalf of his forces. However, the Russians continued to move forward throughout South Ossetian territory, and to unrelentingly engage Georgian Forces wherever they were encountered; accordingly, by the end of August 11th, South Ossetia was completely cleared of Georgian forces, and the Russians, not satisfied with simply defeating the Georgian Armed Forces, continued to move into Georgian territory, to fly sorties against key Georgian targets, and to threaten to replace the Georgian government altogether.

* * * * *

Ryan Madigan departed from his home in Northern Virginia in the early morning hours of August 9th for the two-hour drive to The Monroe Institute. Following his conversation with Colonel Dolidze the night before, he was desperately worried about his brother-in-law, Irakli, and the chance that he might have been wounded, captured or killed in action by the Russians. Since Roin had also shared with him the report that some Georgian SF soldiers had allegedly been placed in detention in a certain, identified jail facility on the northern outskirts of Tskhinvali, Ryan had pondered how he might contribute to the effort to confirm whether Irakli was alive, and if he was actually being detained at that facility. Once Tamara had returned from her work at the hospital, and he broke the unhappy news to her about her brother, he also shared his thoughts with what he might be able to do to assist with locating her brother. After hearing what Ryan had in mind, Tamara broke down into hysterical throes of worry, hugged her husband desperately, and begged him to please do whatever he could.

Upon arrival at The Monroe Institute (TMI) at around 0800, he found his friends waiting for him, his learned instructors of the Out-of-Body Experience (OBE) course he had taken after he left Army service, as well as the former Army veteran and friend who taught and managed the Remote Viewing program. Over coffee, they all convened in the conference room to discuss the full purpose of Ryan's visit, and what role, if any, the TMI staff could play. Although Ryan had been purposefully vague during his telephone discussion the previous evening, he went into full detail now, including the intel he had received the night before from Georgia. As he informed them, his primary purpose was to confirm the location of the Georgian SF POW's, and to confirm their exact numbers, as well as to determine if his brother-in-law was among them. Since, with the guidance of the TMI staff, he had been quite successful in inducing OBE's during the course he had taken with them two years prior, he was there to request their assistance once again, this time with the intention to induce an OBE to conduct an important mission; the lives of his former Georgian SF colleagues, and possibly of his brother-in-law, might be at stake.

The discussion among the small assembled group was animated and intense. Ryan had explained what he had been advised of the alleged location of his Georgian SF comrades, possibly including his brother-in-law, and his desire to conduct an OBE to confirm their location and determine their welfare. The TMI team had listened attentively, and had debated the possibility of successfully conducting such a mission. From his previous OBE experiences during his course, the TMI experts had come to realize that Ryan was one of their most successful students in his proven ability to induce an OBE; he had been clearly helped by his vivid recollection of his initial, involuntary OBE in which he had visited with his father in the spiritual realm. In addition, unlike many OBE students, Ryan did not have an inherent fear of being able to re-enter the physical body following an OBE, since he had experienced that phenomenon several times already. After their lengthy discussion had concluded, influenced greatly by Ryan's plea that time was off the essence, the TMI team unanimously agreed to assist.

They moved immediately to the lab which contained all of the necessary furnishings and equipment for conducting an out-of-body experience. Since they already knew the alleged physical location where the Georgian soldiers were imprisoned, they first confirmed the exact location of the "militsia" (police) station where the Georgians were supposedly being kept by using google earth and other available research in order to define the precise building. Then Ryan took his place in the comfortable recliner; aided by TMI's proprietary sound technology engineered to relax him and bring him into a deep meditative state, the TMI control officer talked him into the proper state of relaxation. Ryan was then asked to concentrate on his recollections of his OBE encounter with his father, to give himself up confidently to the beauty of the spiritual universe, and to allow the release of his spirit into another such journey. Moments later, Ryan consciously found himself looking down upon his physical body, and those of his TMI team. The spiritual journey had begun.

With his purpose fully in mind, and knowing his intended destination, Ryan then found himself entering a tunnel of light much like he recalled from the meeting with his father. He was spirited through a dazzling dimension of energy and light which he knew would ultimately bring him to the planned destination, thousands of earth miles from where his inert body was comfortably positioned. He could not fathom how fast his spiritual essence was being transported, nor how much earth time was passing, but the pure beauty and majesty of the experience held him in a state of ecstatic wonder. Soon, he knew inherently that he was reaching his intended destination; at the end of the tunnel of light, he then suddenly found himself inside of what seemed to be the militsia station on the northern outskirts of Tskhinvali. There below him, crouched on the floor of his jail cell, was his brother-in-law, Irakli.

From Ryan's spiritual viewing point, Irakli seemed to be in good health, although clearly despondent; he wished that he could reach out to Irakli and comfort him, to assure him that all would be well, but he knew that this was not possible. From there, Ryan moved about the prison to try to ascertain how many other Georgian soldiers were present in the building; he was able to identify another 5 men, all seemingly healthy but equally distressed by their uncertain situation. Ryan also reconnoitered the entire station and to determine how many police officials were on duty as a vital part of his mission there. He then returned to Irakli's cell, and took one last long look upon his brother-in-law, allowing himself to concentrate on the love that he and Tamara felt for him. Then, with his mission accomplished, he began to picture his own body, lying in its meditative state, thousands of miles away in the Virginia countryside; as expected, he then found himself re-entering the astral plane, inside the magnificent tunnel of light for the return journey home.

With no concept of how much time had passed on his trip through the astral plane, Ryan soon found himself back in the TMI lab, in full view of his inert body; he then made the conscious decision to re-enter his physical presence. He could immediately feel the warmth of his body enveloping him, and he could hear the voice of his TMI guide talking him through the OBE process. Aware that there was a change in Ryan's physical demeanor, indicating that Ryan had returned, the guide then instructed him to awaken. Ryan drowsily began to assume consciousness; the process of reverting to his physical reality did require a minute or so, and then there was the challenge of consciously absorbing his recollection of the amazing experience he had just concluded. The TMI guide was quite used to this necessity, and he continued patiently to talk Ryan through the process.

Once Ryan had finally recognized his complete return to physical reality, he was anxious to relate the details of what he had experienced and what he had seen at the destination site. The TMI group patiently listened to Ryan's explanation of his magnificent journey; they had heard many such versions before, and they endeavored to help Ryan to focus on the details of his intended mission. Even these TMI OBE professionals were impressed with the amount of exacting detail that Ryan was able to describe, which they were audio recording as part of the process. Once Ryan had completed his rendition of the OBE experience, and it was all recorded, he then needed to decide how best to make use of the information that he had derived. He knew that he needed to report to Roin what he knew about the status of the Georgian soldiers in captivity; the challenge would be to explain how he had come upon such information in a manner that would be believable. Needless to say, the idea of intentionally inducing one's spirit to separate from the body and to make a journey halfway across the globe and back again within a matter of minutes, might come across as a wee bit incredible. As a result, Ryan needed to create a scenario which, at least on the surface, would be more believable.

By the time Ryan had succeeded in reaching Roin, it was around 7:00 pm Tbilisi time on the evening of August 9th. Ryan explained that he had something very important to relay to Roin, but, since they were both using unencrypted cell phones, they understood that the conversation would need to be intentionally vague. Ryan explained that he had confirmed from some undisclosed "former colleagues" that the intel about the Georgian captives was accurate; he confirmed that the number of captives whom they had discussed previously was 6, and that there seemed to be only 3 officials watching them. Roin was surprised that Ryan was able to learn those facts, and wondered how he did it, but expressed gratitude for the information. Roin then said that they had "developed some plans to travel there, very soon," and that it was very useful to know how many people they would meet. Ryan concluded by asking Roin to let him know how his trip went, and the conversation ended. He knew that the information he had been able to convey would be useful, but he fervently wished that he could be there in person to participate in whatever mission Roin had planned. In the physical realm, however, a trip to Tbilisi would require at least 36 hours, which would probably be too late.

Around noon, Ryan thanked his good friends at TMI for their help, and then left for the return trip to Northern Virginia, where his wife would be anxiously awaiting his return. He did call her before leaving TMI to advise that his trip had been successful, that he could inform her now that Irakli was alive and well, and that he would give her the full details when he got home. Two hours later, Ryan pulled into his driveway, and Tamara rushed out to meet him; they desperately embraced and Tamara allowed her tears to flow. Ryan tried to console her, and then he led her inside, where he could explain the full details of his time at TMI, what he had seen in the OBE state, and what he had conveyed to the Georgian SF Commander. After her sense of amazement had dissipated, and all of her many questions were answered, Ryan and Tamara realized that they had done everything they could do; now, the only remaining task was to relax, wait and pray for the best.

* * * * *

The plan that Colonel Dolidze had devised to covertly enter South Ossetia and to rescue their imprisoned Special Forces soldiers was risky at best. In these late evening hours of August 9th, almost 48 hours after they had first infiltrated their two SF detachments into South Ossetian territory, the situation had drastically changed. During these past two days, tens of thousands of Russian soldiers and massive supplies of weapons and equipment had arrived. The fight between Georgian and combined Ossetian and Russian forces had also begun to move strongly to the advantage of the Russian side, and Georgians were methodically being pushed out of South Ossetia back into Georgian Territory. All of the main roads into Ossetia from the southern borders with Georgia were being manned by joint Ossetian-Russian forces, so access into the breakaway republic was greatly constricted. However, Georgian reconnaissance had reported back to HQS that two border crossings east of the Ossetian city of Akhalgori, near the villages of Delkani and Salbieri, did not seem to be manned around the clock; Dolidze believed that it might be possible to make a crossing of the border east of Akhalgori, and to take a circuitous route from there to the northern part of Tskhinvali, while avoiding the larger population centers in-between. And, even though travel would mostly be on largely unpaved, back roads, they estimated that they should be able to make that trek in less than three hours.

The 6-man rescue detachment departed from SF Brigade HQs at 2300 hours, just before midnight, on the night of August 9th. They were travelling in a vegetable delivery van, with two men dressed in working attire in the driver and passenger seats, and the other 4 soldiers hidden in the back of the van, concealed by crates of vegetables. About 90 minutes later, they had reached the border crossing at Salbieri, which, as predicted, they found to be unmanned; the gate was secured with a lock and chain, but a pair of bolt cutters quickly took care of that obstacle. By 0030 on the morning of August 10th, they were driving into Ossetian territory.

The van would need to pass through Akhalgori, but could then take back roads from there to an area north of Tskhinvali, from where they could drive to the jailhouse where their comrades were being held. The goal was to arrive at the jail by 0300, where they anticipated that they would encounter no more than 2 or 3 guards who might be awake; if they were fortunate, they could quickly take control of the facility, free their Georgian comrades, tie up, silence and lock up the Ossetian policemen, and then get back to the border crossing before it was scheduled to re-open at 0600.

The van pulled up outside of the Tskhinvali militsia station #1 at about 0240 in the early morning. All seemed quiet in the area of the station. With the driver and his co-driver keeping guard outside of the station, the other 4 Georgian SF soldiers made their way out of the van, and stealthily moved towards the station entrance. Peeking inside of the front station windows, there appeared to be only one policeman on duty, and he seemed to be fighting sleep. No one else was apparent, although it was assumed that one or two other officers might be sleeping somewhere within. At the moment the leader made the signal to enter, the team quickly and quietly moved inside the double doors. Two members of the team moved quickly toward the policeman at the duty desk, pointed their AK47 assault rifles into his face, and warned him to remain still and quiet. He wisely abided by the warning. The team leader asked him if there were other police officers there, and he pointed towards the back of the station. The other two Georgians then quietly moved from the front lobby towards the back of the station; in one small room behind the lobby, they found another policeman, peacefully sleeping, and they awakened him with the shock of a hand over his mouth and two rifles pointed at his face. There were only two officers on duty.

With everything under control for the moment, and the two police officers quickly and easily rendered defenseless, the team leader then directed the officer at the front desk to show him where the Georgian soldiers were being kept. He showed them to the cell block at the rear of the building, and they all, the 4 Georgians and two Ossetian policemen, entered together; upon entering, two of the Georgians quickly took a head count and confirmed that, as they had been advised, 6 Georgian prisoners were there. One of the policemen was ordered to unlock the cells, and all 6 Georgians were freed; the policemen were then put in separate cells, had their hands tied behind their back, legs secured to the bunks at the rear of the cell, and their mouths were taped securely shut. They were each then quieted with a rifle butt to the head, and left to dream in peace while their cells were locked, and the Georgians made their way back to the van for their escape.

Once placed in the back of the van along with their comrades, the newly-liberated Georgians were ecstatic and thanked their liberators profusely. The team leader quickly took control, gave them weapons which had been brought along, and, as the van departed the area of the police station, he briefed the freed soldiers on what lay ahead. It was already about 0315 as they departed, they had a two-hour plus trip ahead of them, and they needed to reach the border crossing before the gate guards arrived at some time before 0600. In the meantime, they needed to drive undetected through a war zone, avoid any Russian check points along the way, and then get through the border post, all the while being alert and prepared for a firefight at any point along the way.

After having spent the last 60+ hours in detention, and

having been interrogated several times by Russian Spetsnaz soldiers under the threat of bodily harm, or worse, Irakli felt that a huge weight had been lifted from his shoulders. Whereas he knew very well that the road ahead would still be perilous, and that, if captured, the Russians might not be so merciful with them this time, he allowed himself to relax for a moment. He permitted himself to think that, with a little luck and a continuation of God's blessing, he might be back in Tbilisi within a few hours with the opportunity to embrace his beautiful fiance once more. After many hours of desperation, with the realization of his imminent death facing him directly, Irakli had once again found the freedom to hope, and he was fully prepared to fight for it.

Chapter XI:

When the SF rescue team had departed the militsia station with their comrades safely in tow, the detachment commander had sent a brief sitrep to their HQs stating that the first stage of the mission had been successful without incident. He reported that, to his knowledge, the rescue mission had gone undetected, and would remain so until someone entered the police station; the other concern was that the time available to get back to the border crossing before the guards reappear might be insufficient. He requested that support troops be ready and available to assist in the event that they need to fight their way back through the border. Since this had already been written into the mission contingency plan, and a team of Georgian quick reaction forces had already been positioned in the nearby Georgian town of Tsigriantkari, the order immediately went forth to deploy the quick reaction forces to the border to support the rescue mission.

During the ride towards the border crossing at Salbieri, the detachment commander debriefed the soldiers who had been imprisoned; the primary concern was their knowledge, if any, of those SF Team members who had been wounded or killed. Those who had been on the detachment attempting to impede traffic through the Roki Tunnel, confirmed that five of their team members had been killed, and that three more had been wounded in action; they were not aware of where they might have been taken for medical treatment. As for the recon detachment, Irakli reported that two had been wounded in action, and that he had inquired of the jail attendants where his wounded comrades had been taken.

Whereas he did not get a direct response, the policeman had stated that there was only one hospital in Tskhinvali, and he had not volunteered any additional information.

The detachment commander also briefed them on the status of the fighting since they had been inserted into South Ossetia in the early morning hours of August 8th. He informed them that initial Georgian incursions into South Ossetia in and around the city of Tskhinvali had been successful, but that the massive influx of Russian ground forces, artillery and air support had begun to turn the tide of the battle against the Georgian forces. He also reported that Georgian forces were still fighting hard despite the superior numbers and strength of their adversaries, but that the Russian Air Force had begun flying bombing missions into Georgian territory, including against Georgian military bases in the area around Tbilisi. In short, he reported the overall situation was not looking very good, but that their sole mission at present was to get their comrades home safely, which they intended to do.

By just before 0500, two squads of the Georgian quick reaction forces from Tsigriantkari had assumed their positions around the border crossing at Salbieri; their force included two sniper teams, who placed themselves in concealed positions with unobstructed line-of-sight to the border post, a concealed machine gun emplacement at a range of 100 meters, and two four-man detachments positioned in close proximity to the border post in the event they needed to intervene. At 0500, a message was transmitted by the rescue team to HQs, and then promptly relayed to the quick reaction force commander, that the SF jail rescue mission team had just passed through the village of Kanchaveti, about 20 minutes northwest of Akhalgori; it added that, if they could avoid trouble enroute, their ETA at the border crossing would be minutes before 0600. God willing, they might get there before the border guards, but it would certainly be close.

The South Ossetian border detachment for the crossing at Salbieri consisted of two 4-man teams, who would each work 9-hour shifts, from 0600 to 1500, and from 1500 to midnight. The border crossing would be closed and locked between the hours of midnight and 0600. Due to the remoteness of the area, and the poor quality of roads between Georgia and the mostly rural region of Akhalgori, there was generally very little traffic through this border crossing. Prior to the beginning of the conflict on August 8th, there might normally be several Georgian farmers taking their produce across the border to market in Akhalgori, but the war had caused a halt to cross-border commerce. Since the beginning of the conflict, there had been some discussion within the South Ossetian border security department that remote border crossings such as Salbieri should be manned on a 24-hour basis, but nothing had been enacted by the morning of August 10th. The border crossing guards all lived in or around Akhalgori, and the 4-man teams would usually assemble 30 minutes early to travel together to the crossing, normally arriving there several minutes prior to the opening time. On this day, they would arrive there early.

Upon arriving at the border post, the guards all had their normal checklist of duties, opening the office, setting up administratively for the day's activities, and then unlocking the gate. This morning, their activities were under the surveillance of the Georgian quick reaction force commander, who, at 0550, sent a brief situation report message to HQs that the border guards had arrived before the rescue team had gotten through. This information was immediately relayed to the rescue team commander, who in turn briefed his team to ready them for possible action at the border post; as the commander then messaged back to HQs, their van was only about 8 minutes away from the border.

Knowing that the border guards would soon determine that the gate had been breeched during the evening hours, and knowing that the rescue van was only minutes away, the quick reaction force commander decided to take pre-emptive action. He signaled his two four-man teams, who were emplaced in close proximity to the border crossing, to move in and to neutralize the guard force. One team had been instructed to take control of and neutralize the admin shack, and the other to take physical control of the gate and to neutralize any resistance. Within minutes, the teams were in position to act.

Once two of the guards had left the admin shack to proceed to open the gate, the quick reaction force went into action; one team moved quietly and swiftly towards the admin shack, while the other team laid in wait close to the gate. At the moment that the guards reached the gate, and one of them had noticed that the lock had been cut, the 4 Georgians lying in wait emerged with weapons drawn catching the guards completely by surprise. At that same moment, with one man remaining outside to watch for oncoming traffic, three men from the other team entered the admin shack and attained the same result. The border guards, well accustomed to their regular and uneventful morning duties, were quite shocked to find themselves surrounded, with automatic weapons pointed directly at them, and they offered no resistance whatsoever.

The quick reaction force commander messaged HQs that the border crossing had been neutralized, and this information was then forwarded to the rescue team. Since the van was within a kilometer of the border crossing when the message arrived, the timing could not have been more fortuitous. While the quick reaction forces were securing the border crossing, seizing the guards' weapons, and securely immobilizing them, the van with the rescue team and their newly-freed passengers arrived. After a brief conversation with the quick reaction forces, the van continued through the border crossing into Georgian territory for the ride back to Tbilisi. Meanwhile, the quick reaction forces finished securing the border post so as to ensure themselves of sufficient time to depart the area before Ossetian authorities became alerted by the lack of standard communication from Salbieri.

Despite the discomfort of riding for hours inside the van, usually on bumpy unpaved roads, accompanied by the constant anxiety of possible detection and attack by their adversaries, once back within Georgia, Irakli and his teammates could finally breathe a sigh of relief. Irakli's thoughts went immediately to his fiancé, and the anticipated joy of seeing her again soon, and to seeing his beloved family. With his nation in the midst of a full-fledged war with Russia, he knew not what the future would hold; however, with his experiences of these last few days, dominated with the fear and uncertainty of war all around him, Irakli allowed his mind only to concentrate on loving thoughts of family and his prayer that life would soon return to some sense of normalcy. With this temporary feeling of peace enveloping his being, Irakli finally dozed off to sleep for the first time in days.

* * * * *

Just two days after Irakli and his comrades were rescued from Tskhinvali, hostilities between Georgia and Russia officially ended. The results of this five-day conflict had worked to the clear disadvantage of Georgia. Although casualties during the war were fairly equally spread among all participants, Georgia was largely humiliated and had suffered international condemnation; South Ossetia and Abkhazia essentially fell under complete Russian control, and the administration of Georgian President Mikheil Saakhashvili began to slowly unravel. Nevertheless, by the end of August, a tentative sense of peace had once again fallen over this beautiful land, as the Russian "Big Brother" withdrew the vast majority of his forces back into Russian territory.

A few weeks later, on Wednesday, September 17th, 2008, Ryan and Tamara Madigan departed from Dulles International Airport on a Turkish Airlines flight to Istanbul; from there, they would board a connecting flight the following afternoon bound for Tbilisi. They were traveling to attend Irakli's wedding on Saturday, September 20th, which had been postponed several weeks due to a "minor disruption of civility" with Russia and Irakli's call to active duty.

The wedding was to be held at the oldest Georgian Orthodox Church in the country, the Anchiskhati Basilica of Saint Mary, built in Tbilisi in the 6th century. But, in typical

Georgian fashion, the festivities began in earnest several days earlier. To celebrate the return of Tamara and Ryan from the USA, a family supra was held at a favorite restaurant in nearby Mtskheta; most family members were in attendance, including the family matriarch, Ksenia. She had been in poor health these past few months, exacerbated by the recent conflict with Russia, and her deep concern for the safety of her grandson, Irakli. Nevertheless, Ksenia took an active role in the festivities; she especially spent a considerable amount of time catching up with her granddaughter, Tamara, as well as with Irakli and his bride-to-be.

Ksenia also spent some quality one-on-one time with Ryan that evening. She was especially interested to hear Ryan's update on married life in America with her beloved granddaughter, and her insightful questions seemed particularly penetrating. Although Ryan had never revealed the role that he had played in Irakli's liberation from Tskhinvali, nor did he have any intention to do so, Ksenia seemed to intuitively understand that he had somehow been of assistance. With each of her delving questions, the twinkle in her vibrant eyes and her seemingly knowing smile indicated to Ryan that, inexplicably, she was somehow aware of his involvement, and that she was silently extending her deep gratitude for what he had done for her family. After returning to their hotel that evening, Ryan asked Tamara if Ksenia had somehow found out about his involvement in Irakli's rescue; Tamara chuckled, and replied to the negative, adding only that Baba Ksenia always seemed to understand the truth without needing to be told.

Family activities dominated the following day as well, but Ryan took the time to visit with his American colleagues still working for the Georgian Ministry of Defense, and with his friends at the Georgian Special Forces Brigade, including a lengthy meeting with Colonel Dolidze. Although Roin attempted to probe several times how Ryan had known about the number and condition of their captives in Tskhinvali, Ryan simply grinned and blamed his inability to discuss the details with the normal "sources and methods" disclaimer. All of the captive team members were also invited to join them for a drink and a special toast to Ryan's undisclosed assistance, for which they all expressed their fervent gratitude.

The wedding on Saturday was a typically traditional Georgian affair. The service at the Basilica was a beautiful orthodox service, and the ambiance of the 6th century cathedral was nothing short of holy. The singing of The Divine Liturgy was reminiscent to Ryan of his Roman Catholic upbringing, yet transported him mentally back through the centuries of this rich Georgian Orthodox tradition. The extended family and dozens of guests took part in the service, and all fully appreciated the good fortune and grace that had allowed this fateful event to transpire. No one was seemingly more entranced than Ksenia; she stood in apparent peace and wonderment as the young couple made their commitment to their future life together. The service was certainly a fitting and happy conclusion to the fear and uncertainty of the tragic weeks that had just passed.

The reception following the wedding was predictably festive, and Irakli's father, the Tamada for the supra, was especially eloquent and justifiably emotional as he worked through the dozens of toasts celebrating the nation, the soldiers who had so bravely served their motherland, the souls of their ancestors, and the many blessings of the young married couple. In typical Georgian fashion, the feast was enormous and the wine consumption exceeded what normal human beings might be expected to handle. For Ryan and Tamara, the day had been truly exultant, and both departed from the event happily well-fed, and slightly intoxicated, both from the many goblets of Georgian wine and from the sense of happiness that enveloped them.

Ryan felt especially gratified that he had the opportunity to spend more quality time with Ksenia; despite her poor health, she had reveled in the day's festivities, and Ryan had the sense she was fully aware that future family opportunities such as this might be limited. Throughout the day, she had appeared ebullient yet somewhat pensive in her demeanor, as if she was savoring every moment of this blessed event. In fact, as they departed Tbilisi the next day for their long trek home to the United States, this would be the last time that Ryan and Tamara would see Ksenia alive.

Epilogue:

Ksenia Kolumbegovi passed away peacefully in her sleep on May 1st, 2009, at the age of 85. Her two sons were with her at her bedside when she exhaled her final breath. Tamara and Ryan were informed shortly thereafter with a phone call from her father. Although Ksenia's passing had been expected, Tamara was predictably inconsolable; she felt quite guilty that her work at the hospital had prevented her from flying home to be with Ksenia in her final days. Trying to comfort her, Ryan spent the evening late into the morning hours holding his beloved wife, and allowing her emotions to dissipate as her feeling of grief gradually eased in intensity. They rarely spoke, but, when they did, it was to bring up memories of Ksenia and the legacy of her remarkable life.

Ryan recalled what his favorite history professor at Georgetown University had said during one of his lectures, "a person's legacy largely depends upon the realities of the times in which they lived." Ryan often thought about the truth contained in the professor's statement, and how it had so accurately pertained to his parents' lives, and, even though far from complete, his own life. He mentioned that phrase to Tamara that evening, and elaborated with his reflections of what realities Ksenia had faced during her lifetime, and how she had fared.

Born soon following the Russian Revolution and the birth of the USSR, with her father having served in the Tsarist Army during World War I before becoming one of the founding generation of the Communist Party in Georgia,

Ksenia's life journey had certainly experienced the full range of tumultuous times. She had entered this world during political and economic uncertainty, grown up during extreme periods of totalitarianism, in which frequent political assassinations expanded into mass purges of anyone suspected of opposition, and married in the midst of history's deadliest conflict, World War II. During the formative years of raising her own family, with the country suffering through post-war scarcities exacerbated by the ill-fated precepts of the communist economic model, she had used her survival instincts and creativity to discover her own entrepreneurial spirit which enabled her to provide well for her family. And, in the autumn of her life, she had been blessed to witness the end of 70 years of communism, political independence, and the eventuality of a free and democratic Georgian nation, in which her grandchildren and great-grandchildren might grow and prosper within a less tumultuous environment.

Ksenia's life clearly could not have spanned a more challenging period of human history, yet she had never allowed external factors to deter her from living a full existence. By every measure of life, she had clearly succeeded well beyond all reasonable expectations, and had lived her life practicing the Christian principles that the atheist state had tried to bury. In a time when the Soviet government glorified those who allegedly brought credit to the state with such medals as "Hero of the Soviet Union" or "Hero of Socialist Labor," Ksenia genuinely personified the true heroes of her time. She had not only survived the tumult, but prospered. She had dedicated her impressive energies to her loved ones, and, by doing so, had raised several generations of bright and talented individuals who had already brought great credit to the motherland, and would for many generations to come.

Motivated by the life-changing spiritual events that he had experienced, Ryan had become an avid aficionado of metaphysical subject matter, and had delved deeply into the topic of reincarnation and those "old souls" who seemed to live among us. Ryan's impressions of Ksenia had always fed his belief that she must truly be an old soul, blessed with the inherent wisdom and loving spirit of those who have learned the important lessons of life during multiple manifestations. From the time of their first meeting just a few years prior, Ryan had immediately known that Ksenia was a special person; he could see the source of wisdom in the depth of her eyes, and literally feel the bounteous nature of her love in the knowing ease of her smile and the magnetic energy that she generated. Yes, Ryan had whispered to Tamara, Ksenia was truly one of those all-too-rare people who is truly special and forever memorable; and the love and wisdom with which she blessed her loved ones will never be forgotten. "After all," he said, "she will always be with us in spirit whenever we need her, just as my father has been for me; all we need to do is ask for her guidance, and it shall be given."

Author's Notes:

As mentioned in the disclaimer at the beginning of the book, this novella is intended as a work of historical fiction. The historical framework into which the story has been written is largely accurate, although certain specific events within that framework have been created for the sake of the story.

The Monroe Institute (TMI) does exist, and it does offer programs as mentioned within this book. For information on TMI, please refer to their web site at www.monroeinstitute. org.

Ksenia Kolumbegovi did in fact exist, and the story contained herein is largely based on her life story. The author did have the privilege to meet her, and her story as written closely follows family legacy. Ksenia Kolumbegovi was indeed an incredible human being, and it is an honor to share her remarkable story with the readers of this novella.

The Georgian Beekeeper is the first book in The Ryan Madigan Series, of which there will be several subsequent publications; Ryan Madigan is a fictional character, although he may bear some accidental similarities to people whom this author has been privileged to know during his lifetime.

The author hopes that you have enjoyed this humble story, and that you will stayed tuned for more to follow. Meanwhile, best wishes!

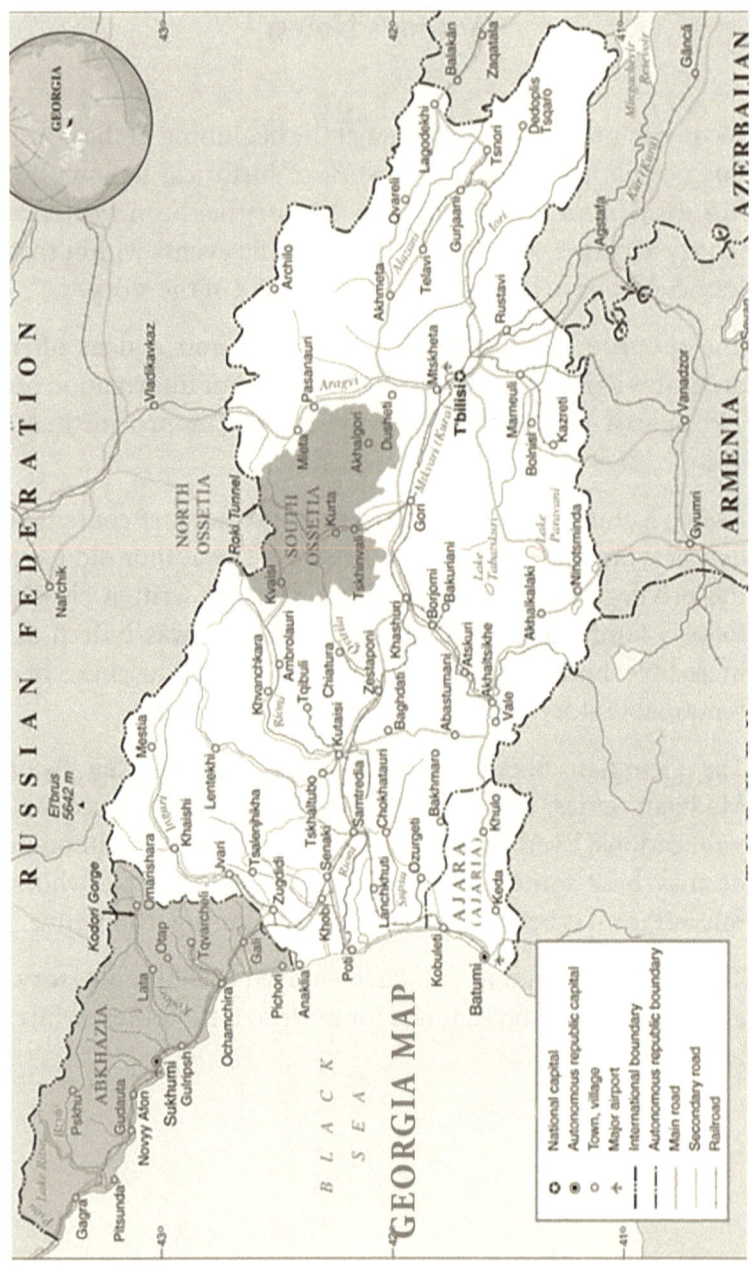

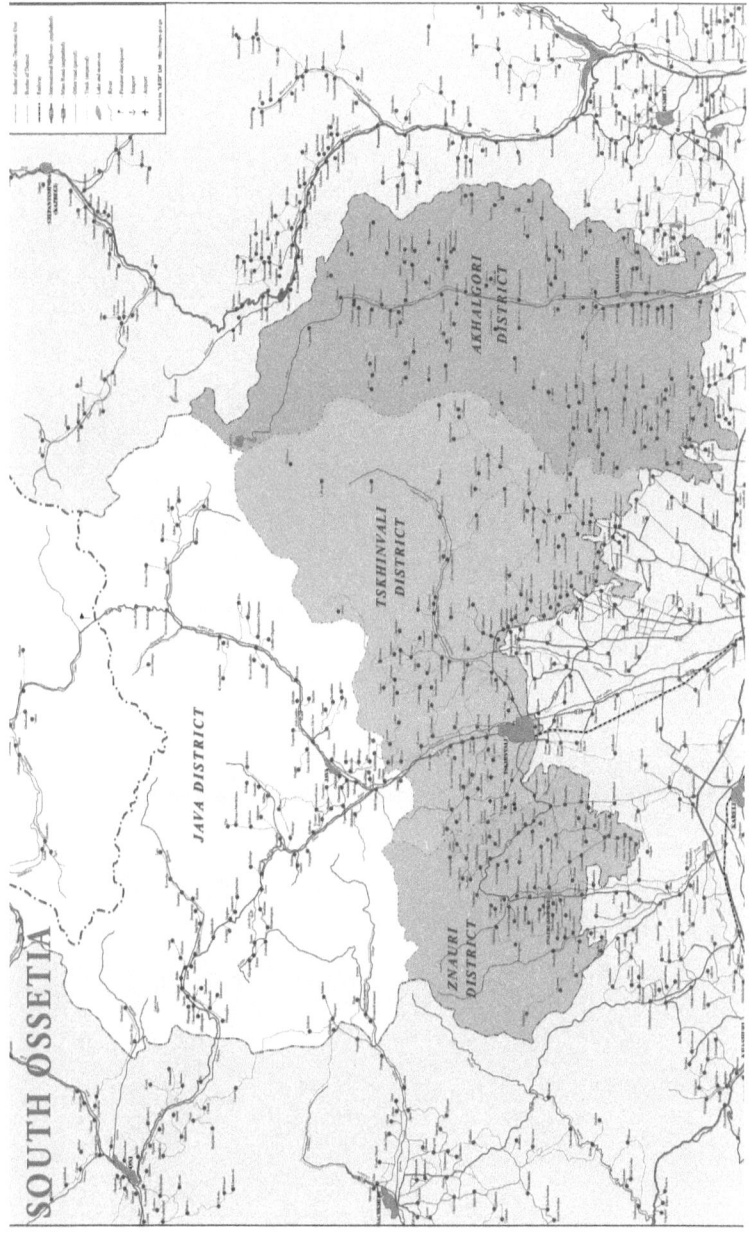